A DOCTOR'S VOW (SE #1293)
by Christine Rimmer,
on sale December 1999

THEIR LITTLE PRINCESS (SE #1298)
by Susan Mallery,
on sale January 2000

DR. MOM AND THE MILLIONAIRE
(SE #1304)
by Christine Flynn,
on sale February 2000

Despite her best intentions, Kelly felt her heart opening to both this man and this child.

Tanner was the kind of man women dreamed about. Not just because he was handsome, but because he was strong and kind and caring. He'd taken Lia, even knowing he was going to be a single father. He'd lacked both skills and practical knowledge. He'd been terrified, but he'd done it anyway.

And somehow, when she wasn't paying attention, Kelly had intertwined both her life and her heart with the pair and she didn't know how to separate them.

She was in no ⌷⌷⌷⌷⌷⌷⌷⌷⌷⌷⌷ one right now.

Still, she knew ⌷⌷⌷⌷⌷⌷⌷⌷⌷⌷⌷ special man. And although she wasn't ready, if she wanted to keep him in her life, she was going to have to do something about *getting* ready.

Dear Reader,

It's going to be a wonderful year! After all, we're celebrating Silhouette's 20th anniversary of bringing you compelling, emotional, contemporary romances month after month.

January's fabulous lineup starts with beloved author Diana Palmer, who returns to Special Edition with *Matt Caldwell: Texas Tycoon*. In the latest installment of her wildly popular LONG, TALL TEXANS series, temperatures rise and the stakes are high when a rugged tycoon meets his match in an innocent beauty—who is also his feisty employee.

Bestselling author Susan Mallery continues the next round of the series PRESCRIPTION: MARRIAGE with *Their Little Princess*. In this heart-tugging story, baby doctor Kelly Hall gives a suddenly single dad lessons in parenting—and learns all about romance!

Reader favorite Pamela Toth launches Special Edition's newest series, SO MANY BABIES—in which babies and romance abound in the Buttonwood Baby Clinic. In *The Baby Legacy*, a sperm-bank mix-up brings two unlikely parents together temporarily—or perhaps forever....

In Peggy Webb's passionate story, *Summer Hawk*, two Native Americans put aside their differences when they unite to battle a medical crisis and find that love cures all. Rounding off the month is veteran author Pat Warren's poignant, must-read secret baby story, *Daddy by Surprise*, and Jean Brashear's *Lonesome No More*, in which a reclusive hero finds healing for his heart when he offers a single mom and her young son a haven from harm.

I hope you enjoy these six unforgettable romances and help us celebrate Silhouette's 20th anniversary all year long!

Best,

Karen Taylor Richman
Senior Editor

Please address questions and book requests to:
Silhouette Reader Service
U.S.: 3010 Walden Have., P.O. Box 1325, Buffalo, NY 14269
Canadian: P.O. Box 609, Fort Erie, Ont. L2A 5X3

SUSAN MALLERY
THEIR LITTLE PRINCESS

SPECIAL EDITION®

Published by Silhouette Books
America's Publisher of Contemporary Romance

To Christine Flynn and Christine Rimmer,
for letting me "ride along" a second time.
This was great fun and I hope we can do it again real soon.
And to my editor, Karen Taylor Richman,
who believed in this project
from the beginning.

 SILHOUETTE BOOKS

ISBN 0-373-24298-0

THEIR LITTLE PRINCESS

Copyright © 2000 by Susan W. Macias

Visit us at www.romance.net

Printed in U.S.A.

Books by Susan Mallery

*Hometown Heartbreakers
†Triple Trouble
§Montana Mavericks: Return to Whitehorn
‡Brides of Bradley House

SUSAN MALLERY

is the bestselling author of over thirty books for
Silhouette. Always a fan of romance novels, Susan finds
herself in the unique position of living out her own personal romantic fantasy with the new man in her life.
Susan lives in sunny California with her handsome hero
husband and her two adorable but not-bright cats.

IT'S OUR 20th ANNIVERSARY!
We'll be celebrating all year, starting with these fabulous titles, on sale in January 2000.

Special Edition

 #1297 Matt Caldwell: Texas Tycoon
Diana Palmer

 #1298 Their Little Princess
Susan Mallery

 #1299 The Baby Legacy
Pamela Toth

#1300 Summer Hawk
Peggy Webb

#1301 Daddy by Surprise
Pat Warren

#1302 Lonesome No More
Jean Brashear

Intimate Moments

 #979 Murdock's Last Stand
Beverly Barton

 #980 Marrying Mike... Again
Alicia Scott

#981 A Drive-By Wedding
Terese Ramin

 #982 Midnight Promises
Eileen Wilks

#983 The Comeback of Con MacNeill
Virginia Kantra

 #984 Witness... and Wife?
Kate Stevenson

Romance

 #1420 The Baby Bequest
Susan Meier

#1421 With a Little T.L.C.
Teresa Southwick

#1422 The Sheik's Solution
Barbara McMahon

 #1423 Annie and the Prince
Elizabeth Harbison

#1424 A Babe in the Woods
Cara Colter

#1425 Prim, Proper... Pregnant
Alice Sharpe

Desire

 #1267 Her Forever Man
Leanne Banks

 #1268 The Pregnant Princess
Anne Marie Winston

 **#1269 Dr. Mommy**
Elizabeth Bevarly

 #1270 Hard Lovin' Man
Peggy Moreland

#1271 The Cowboy Takes a Bride
Cathleen Galitz

#1272 Skyler Hawk: Lone Brave
Sheri WhiteFeather

Chapter One

"You're going to tell me that I'm crazy," Tanner Malone said as he paced the length of his brother's office. "Maybe I am. Maybe I've been working too hard, or maybe it's because I'm going to be forty in three years. I don't know why I have to do this, I just know that I do."

He paused in the center of the office and stared at his brother, Ryan, who sat behind his large wooden desk. "You're not saying anything," Tanner told him. "Don't you want to talk me out of this?"

Ryan gave an easy, familiar smile. "I've got three kids already, and another one on the way. Who am I to advise anyone against fatherhood? You might find that you like it."

Tanner nodded once, then collapsed into the leather chair opposite Ryan's. "Fatherhood," he muttered under his breath. "I *am* crazy. What do I know about being a father?"

"You're a great uncle, if that helps. My kids adore you. All kids adore you. For that matter, women seem to find you irresistible. I'll bet that puppies and kittens follow you around, too."

Tanner didn't have to glance at his older brother's face to know that Ryan was kidding him. "This is serious," he said. "I have to make a decision."

"I know you do, and I'll give you whatever information you want, it's just…" Ryan shrugged. "I can't help it, Tanner. For years you made fun of my boring married life, all the while being the carefree bachelor. You've gone through girlfriends like most guys go through a six pack of beer over Super Bowl weekend. You gave it a good race, but someone finally caught you."

"So what you're saying is I'm due." Tanner didn't like the sound of that, but he wasn't sure his brother was wrong. He'd avoided paying for his lifestyle for a long time. But in the next twenty-four hours, that was all going to change.

"I'm pointing out that it's taken you a long time to come to the place where you have to make some difficult choices," Ryan said. "Most men have already gone through this by the time they're your age."

Tanner leaned back in his chair. He knew Ryan was right—about a lot of things. What his older brother *wasn't* saying was that Tanner had occasionally needed to fall on his butt before life or circumstances or whatever got his attention. Well, he was paying attention now. The problem was what to do?

"I don't know how to be a good father," Tanner said as the knot in his stomach went from the size of a baseball to that of a basketball. He felt as if he'd taken a tumble from one of his high-rises and while the fall hadn't killed him, it had sure shaken him up some.

"No one knows anything at the beginning," Ryan said. "You learn by doing."

"What if I mess him up? I don't want my son suffering just because his old man couldn't get the hang of parenting."

"He or *she* needs you to love them and be there. Everything else is negotiable."

Ryan continued talking, but Tanner wasn't listening. His brain had frozen at the sound of a single word. She. Dear God, the baby could be girl! That would be worse. Based on his messed up personal life, the amount he knew about women wouldn't fill a teaspoon.

"She can't have a girl," Tanner said, interrupting Ryan. "I can't have a daughter."

Ryan chuckled. "There's logic. I hate to remind you about this, Tanner, but that decision was made a long time ago. About nine months, to be exact, and the decision was made by you."

Tanner swore under his breath. He glanced at the clock. Lucy had called him two hours before to say she was on her way to the hospital. The mother of his unborn child had long since signed the papers giving the baby up for adoption. Lucy expected him to do the same. It was what they'd agreed to do. It was the smart thing to do. It was what nearly everyone had told him to do. But he hadn't been able to do it. All the logic in the world couldn't make Tanner sign away a life that was a part of him.

He pushed to his feet and headed for the door.

"Where are you going?" Ryan asked.

"To the hospital."

"What are you going to do?"

Tanner gripped the door handle and glanced back at the only family he'd known. His big brother had always been there for him. This time, Tanner was on his own.

"Hell if I know," he said and slammed the door shut behind him.

"Pretty girl," Kelly Hall murmured as she stared down at the squirming newborn she held. "You look so worried, but I promise that we grown-ups know how to take care of you."

Sandy, one of the obstetrics nurses, stroked the infant's cheek. "You tell her, Dr. Hall. But I don't think it's going to help. I've been watching babies being born for over twenty years and every one of them has had that same worried look."

"It's our job to reassure them." Kelly gave "Baby Ames" a last smile, then reluctantly handed her over to Sandy. The competent nurse would take her over to the nursery where, for the next couple of days, she would receive excellent care. As for what would happen after that, who could say. The child was being given up for adoption.

Kelly had long since learned that it wasn't her place to judge her patients or question their nonmedical decisions. Even so she couldn't help glancing at the weary woman about to be wheeled to her room.

"Are you sure you don't want to see your daughter?" she asked one last time.

Lucy Ames, a platinum blonde who managed to look stunning, even after giving birth, rolled her eyes. "Get over it, Doc. I know you were hoping that I would get bitten by the maternal bug when the kid popped out, but it's not gonna happen. I signed the papers a long time ago and I haven't changed my mind. In less than two weeks, I'm heading to L.A. and I'm not coming back. I plan to live in the land of sun and movie stars. The last thing I want in my life is some kid messing everything up."

"I understand," Kelly said politely, even though she didn't. Lucy was a grown woman with options. How could she turn her back on her own child?

"I appreciate everything you did," Lucy told her. "You're good at this."

"It's my job," Kelly said lightly, then slipped off her gloves. "I'll be in to check on you in a few hours. Just to make sure everything is fine. But based on the delivery, you're going to heal quickly."

Lucy gave a little wave as the nurse wheeled her out of the delivery room. Kelly followed more slowly. She thought about the patients she still had to see that day, and about those who would soon be giving birth. Most of her patients were thrilled to be pregnant and anxiously awaited the birth of their new baby. But occasionally she had one like Lucy— a woman to whom giving birth was an inconvenience.

It wasn't that she didn't understand Lucy. In some ways she understood too well. Maybe that's what got to her. Maybe Lucy's situation reminded her too much of her own shortcomings.

Knowing that she should head back to her office, Kelly walked toward the elevator. But instead of pushing the button for the ground floor, she found herself heading over to the nursery. She told herself she just wanted to quickly check on Baby Ames. A complete lie because the pediatrician on duty wouldn't have finished examining her yet.

Regardless of her reasons, twenty minutes later Kelly stood in front of the glass-enclosed nursery. Nearly a dozen babies slept or squirmed in their soft blankets. Pink and blue caps clearly defined gender.

She could see through to the opposite wall where a man stood with his arm around a young woman in a bathrobe. They were both pointing and smiling at a tiny child. The woman wasn't Kelly's patient, but she recognized the slightly stunned glow. Their child had been the couple's first, she thought. As new parents, they were equal parts thrilled and terrified. She knew that over time, love and joy would replace the terror, right up until their baby became a teenager, at which point they would want to pull their hair out.

The thought made her smile. She pressed her hand against the glass and studied the tiny infants. She found three that she'd delivered in the past twenty-four hours, then watched as one of the nurses put Baby Ames into her isolette.

"Let it go," she murmured to herself, knowing there was no point in getting upset or attached. Lucy Ames had made her decision, as was her right. The beautiful baby girl would be given up for adoption. It's not as if she, Kelly, had done any better.

But I was only seventeen, a voice in her head whispered. Didn't that make a difference? Kelly wasn't sure anymore. Maybe she'd never been sure.

"Dr. Hall?"

The low male voice broke through her musings and she turned to face the man who came up to stand beside her.

The overhead lights were bright in the hallway. Even so Kelly blinked several times to make sure she was really seeing who she thought she saw. Tanner Malone.

She thought about cursing him, or simply walking away. She thought about giving him a piece of her mind, then reminded herself it wasn't her business. She was Lucy's doctor, nothing else. Still, for once, she was grateful for her five feet ten inches and the fact that she'd changed out of scrubs and back into a skirt, blouse and heels. With them she could look Mr. Malone in the eye...or almost. His work boots gave him an inch or so on her.

She wondered how he knew her name, then figured it wouldn't have been difficult to track her down. From what Lucy had told her, she and Tanner weren't an item anymore but that didn't mean the couple didn't talk. After all, they'd just brought a child into the world.

Kelly fought against the anger rising inside of her. So what if Tanner Malone was an irresponsible bastard? She could be courteous for a few minutes.

"I'm Dr. Hall," she said.

"Tanner Malone."

She was afraid he was going to hold out his hand for her to shake, but he didn't. Instead he shoved them into his jeans pockets and blew out a deep breath.

"I've been looking all over for you," he admitted. "Now that you're here, I don't know what to say."

"I see." She glanced at her watch. It was nearly noon. Her morning patients would have been rescheduled, but she still had afternoon appointments. "Perhaps when you think of it you can call my office and we'll—"

"No." He grabbed her arm before she could step away. Even through her temper she felt a quick jolt of...something...as his fingers closed around her. Was it heat? Was it—

Don't even think about that, she told herself angrily. How dare her body react in a favorable way toward this man? He was slime. He was lower than slime. He was the single cell creature fifteen million years away from evolving into slime.

"I need to talk to you about the baby." He gestured to the nursery behind them. "I..." He released her. "I want to know what Lucy had. I asked at the desk, but because she already signed the adoption papers they're not giving out information."

He looked tired, Kelly thought irrelevantly. Shadows pooled under impossibly blue eyes. Malone blue, she'd heard a couple of nurses saying a while back. Yeah, he was good-looking. So what? He was still slime.

"I don't understand why anything about the baby is important to you, Mr. Malone," Kelly said crisply. "Once you sign the release forms, the child ceases to be your responsibility."

"That's the thing," he said. "I haven't signed them. I'm not sure I can."

Kelly didn't know if she would have been more surprised if he'd started yapping like a poodle. She felt her mouth drop open, but she couldn't seem to pull her jaw back into place. "What?"

Tanner glanced over his shoulder, then waved toward the corridor. "Is there somewhere we can go to talk for a minute? I'm sorry if I seem out of it, but I haven't had much sleep in the past few weeks. Between the hours I've been working and thinking about the baby, I've been pacing more than I've been sleeping."

She pressed her lips together. Tanner Malone had to be playing some kind of game. A man in his position would never consent to raise a child alone. Still, he'd captured her attention, so she decided to hear him out.

"There are a couple of consultation rooms just down here," she said, leading the way.

They turned left at the nurse's station and paused as Kelly checked the first room. It was unoccupied. She entered, then waited for Tanner to follow her before closing the door.

The room was small, maybe eight by eight, with a desk and three chairs. She moved around Tanner and settled into the single chair behind the desk, then motioned for him to take one of the remaining seats. He glanced at it, then shook his head and paced from the door to the wall. It took him all of three steps.

"The thing is, I know it's crazy," he began, not looking at her, but instead staring at the floor. "The hospital is adding a new wing."

The comment seemed irrelevant until Kelly remembered that Tanner Malone owned the company building the wing. Construction had been going on for months. "Actually, I've noticed that."

"Really?"

He glanced at her, and she was again caught up in the realization that his eyes were really a very deep blue. Forget it, she told herself firmly. Ignore the man, listen to the words.

"Then you probably know that my company is in charge of the construction. It's a huge project, involving thousands of man-hours, not to mention dozens of subcontractors. I'd been working twelve, fourteen-hour days. Then the funding got stalled."

Kelly nodded. For a time it seemed that the new wing wasn't going to open as planned but Ryan Malone, Tanner's brother, had pulled off a miracle.

"Now we're playing catch-up," Tanner continued. "I rarely see my house. We're going to make the September first deadline for the dedication, but it's going to be tight. So I don't have time for a child in my life. Certainly not a baby."

Kelly leaned back against the chair and worked hard to keep her face impassive. So he hadn't been asking about the child at all, she thought grimly. He only wanted to talk to her so that he could explain his case to someone—anyone. He wanted to make excuses. She waited for the anger to return, but it was gone—transformed into a sadness she wasn't sure she could explain.

There were so many hopeful couples wanting to adopt infants. Baby Ames would be placed with a loving family. She might grow up with every advantage. It was probably best for everyone. Kelly drew in a breath. If only she could let this go. Why was this one child getting to her?

"I can't do it," Tanner said.

"Mr. Malone, you don't have to explain this to me, and frankly I'm not interested in your reasons for giving up your child for adoption."

"But that's my point," he said. "I can't do it. I can't give him up." He pulled a thick sheath of papers from his back pocket and dropped them on the desk. "Lucy and I talked about this and we both agreed it was the best thing. She's got a job waiting for her in L.A. and I've got a busy life here. Adoption made sense."

Kelly picked up the sheets and flipped through them. Lucy had carefully signed away all her rights to the child, but the space for Tanner's signature was blank.

"What do you think?" he asked.

She glanced up and saw that Tanner had braced his hands on the back of one of the chairs and leaned toward her. His thick, dark hair fell over his forehead. He wasn't the usual kind of man who populated her day. Most of them were other doctors or husbands of patients. She saw more suits than jeans and workshirts. Tanner might own Malone Construction but he obviously didn't mind getting his hands dirty. She could see scars on his fingers, and there were thick muscles bulging in his upper arms and chest. She nearly matched him in height, but he had to outweigh her by forty pounds, all of them muscle.

"What do I think about what?" she asked.

"What should I do? Should I sign the papers?"

"I can't answer that for you. We're talking about

a child, Mr. Malone. This isn't a decision to be made lightly. Your daughter's future is at stake."

His eyes widened and a grin split his face. If she'd thought he was good-looking before, he was amazingly handsome now. That smile could cause a woman to stumble at fifty paces, she thought refusing to soften toward him.

"A girl!" He sank into the chair, then rubbed his eyes. "Damn. Like I know anything about women."

"You know enough to get one of them pregnant." Kelly regretted the words as soon as they passed her lips. She sighed. "Sorry. I didn't mean to say that."

"Don't apologize. You've got a point." He leaned forward. "Is she okay? Ten fingers and toes?"

Kelly smiled. "She's perfect. A real beauty. Her Apgar score was a nine at one minute and a ten at five minutes." When Tanner looked blank, Kelly explained. "We check newborns for several characteristics right after birth. Their heart rate, whether they are crying, moving around, that sort of thing. Your daughter scored very high. There's every indication that she's healthy and normal."

"A girl," he said, his voice filled with awe. "Jeez. I feel like that changes everything, but I'm not sure it does." He looked at her. "Tell me that the adoption is the best thing. Tell me that I have no business trying to raise a kid on my own. When would I find the time? Tell me I don't know the first thing about babies or children."

"No one can make that decision but you, Mr. Malone."

Tanner nodded. He'd been hoping for a little

guidance from Lucy's doctor, but Kelly Hall wasn't going to be much help there. Based on the look she'd given him when he'd first approached her, she wasn't very pleased with him at all. He wondered if her anger was at him specifically or men in general. Or maybe she didn't like men who welched on their commitments and responsibilities. Could he blame her for that?

"I want to see her," he said. "My daughter, I mean, not Lucy. If I haven't signed the papers, can I do that?"

Some of the tension left Kelly's face. Her full lips curved up in a sweet smile. "I can do better than that, Mr. Malone. I can let you hold her."

"This isn't a good idea," Tanner said ten minutes later as Kelly started to put a tiny wrapped bundle into his arms. "I don't do the baby thing. I sort of ignored my nieces and nephew until they got past the breakable stage."

"She's tougher than she looks," Kelly promised, even though he knew she was lying. "Just relax. Bend your arm so she's completely supported and her head can rest in the crook of your elbow."

The baby was red and kind of squished looking. He couldn't see any part of her except for her face. Even her head was covered with a little pink cap. She was too tiny not to scare the pants off him. And when Kelly placed her in his arms, she seemed to weigh nothing at all.

"Oh, God." He placed his free hand against her side to keep her from slipping and stayed completely still. "She's about the size of a football."

"I'll have to take your word on that."

He glanced up and saw that Kelly was still smiling at him. No doubt she was amused by his stiffness, but he'd never held a newborn before.

"Now what?" he asked.

"Say hello, or anything else that comes to mind. She's your child, Mr. Malone. What would you like to do?"

Give her back, he thought, but he didn't say that. "Call me Tanner."

Kelly chuckled. "Most fathers prefer Daddy."

He glanced at her. "I was talking to you. You keep saying Mr. Malone. I'm Tanner. I'd shake hands, but they're tied up at the moment."

"I understand." She pointed to the baby. "It's okay to move around if you'd like."

He shook his head, too scared to do anything but stand there holding his daughter. Feelings swelled up inside of him, emotions that he could barely identify. There was pride and fear, but so much more. A sense of having been part of a miracle. Was this tiny creature really flesh of his flesh? Had he had some small part in creating her?

Kelly seemed to understand his confusion. She patted his arm, then stepped back to give him time alone.

Tanner took a tentative step, then another. His daughter didn't wake up. He risked a tiny rocking motion. When she stirred, he froze.

Against his arm he felt small movements. His daughter puckered her mouth, then opened her eyes and stared up at him.

She had blue eyes…Malone blue. He remembered reading somewhere that newborns couldn't see all that well, but at that moment it seemed to him that his baby could see into his soul.

Tanner Malone had never been a believer in love at first sight, nor had he ever experienced anything even remotely close to it. But as he stared down at the tiny infant who was his child, he felt himself falling faster and harder than he ever had before in his life.

Chapter Two

Kelly watched the play of emotions across Tanner's face and knew he was a goner. Deep inside, she felt the first flicker of guilt. Maybe it had been wrong to let him hold his daughter. There was something special about holding a newborn. A friend of hers had once described it as one of life's few incredibly perfect moments. She'd allowed Tanner to experience the magic, but what about the reality? Could he handle that?

Kelly told herself that if he hadn't been open to wanting his child, he wouldn't have felt anything while the baby was in his arms, but she wasn't sure she believed that. Was she doing the right thing? Could Tanner Malone handle having a baby in his life? Unfortunately, based on his stunned expression, he no longer had a choice in the matter.

He looked at Kelly, his eyes dark with panic. "I want to keep her. Is that wrong?"

"She's your daughter, Tanner. How can you wanting to raise her be wrong?"

"I can give you about three dozen reasons, starting with the fact that I know less than zero about babies. Then there's the issue of my twenty hour days."

"You'll make it work. Millions of single parents do every day."

He didn't look convinced. "Maybe. So what happens now?"

"Now I notify the hospital that Baby Ames won't be given up for adoption and that her name should be changed to Baby Malone."

Tanner smiled that devastating smile again. Fortunately for Kelly's equilibrium, it was focused on his daughter, not at her. "Did you hear that? You're my little girl and everyone is going to know it. You're Baby Malone."

"You might want to think about getting her a first name," Kelly said dryly. "She's going to find Baby Malone a little difficult when she gets to school."

He nodded. "You're right. So what happens after you tell the hospital?"

"You're going to have to talk to the adoption agency and tell them you've changed your mind. Legally, it's not a problem. If you haven't signed the papers, they can't make you give up your daughter. However, you're still going to need a good lawyer. You'll have to make custody arrangements with Lucy. I'm guessing that if she was willing to give the baby up for adoption she won't want visitation rights, but you'll have to check. There's also the issue of support.'' She frowned. ''There might be more, but a good family lawyer can answer those questions better than I can.''

''Too much to think about,'' he said quietly, still looking at his daughter. ''I don't want anything from Lucy. If she wants to walk away from her daughter, then that's fine with me. I don't need her money.''

''You'll have to work that out with her. She's still in the hospital if you want to talk with her.''

He glanced up. ''She can have visitors?''

''Of course. It was giving birth, not brain surgery. She probably feels like she was run over by a truck, but she's healthy and in great shape. She'll recover quickly. Both she and the baby will be released tomorrow.'' She hesitated and wondered if Tanner had any clue what he was getting into. ''I can ask that your daughter be kept here until the afternoon. That should give you time to arrange things.''

''What kind of things?''

Kelly drew in a deep breath. It was worse than she thought. ''Tanner, have you ever been around a newborn before?''

''No, like I said, I avoided my brother's kids until they were past the breakable stage.''

''I see.'' She wasn't sure how to break the news to him. ''Your life is about to change in a big way. You'll need baby furniture, clothes, formula, diapers, not to mention a couple of good books on dealing with an infant. You're going to have to arrange for child care at home for at least the first couple of weeks. While most day care places will take a newborn at six weeks, you don't want her exposed to a lot of children right now. Young kids have frequent colds, and that's not good news for an infant.''

He took a step back, then another. She saw his muscles tighten, although his hold on the baby stayed relaxed and supportive. "You're saying I don't have a prayer of making this work."

She stared at him, at the too handsome face and the worry in his eyes. She could practically hear the thoughts racing through his mind at light speed.

"Not at all. I'm not trying to scare you, but I do want to point out that this is a little more complicated than making a home for a puppy."

He swore under his breath, then paced to the glass wall in the alcove of the nursery. Kelly ached for his pain and confusion. He had to be scared to death, but she sensed he wasn't going to change his mind about his daughter. Despite her initial dislike of him, she had to respect that. Fifteen years ago, she'd had to make the same choice and in the end, she'd given her daughter away. It had been the hardest thing she'd ever done.

She respected Tanner for wanting to try. Unfortunately, he had several strikes against him. The most significant were a complete lack of knowledge and preparation, and his impossible work schedule. If he had an office job, it might not be too hard to schedule at least a couple of weeks off. But Tanner was the general contractor for the hospital's hundred-million dollar renovation. For reasons that had nothing to do with him, the project was behind schedule. When was he supposed to find the time to take care of his daughter?

"I can help," she blurted out impulsively, then wondered where on earth that thought had come from.

He turned and looked at her. "What do you mean?"

"Just what I said." She glanced at her watch. "Meet me back here at six tonight. It's Friday, so the stores are open late. I'll take you to a baby store, then help you set everything up for her. I'm on call this weekend, but assuming no one gives birth, I can even be around to give you pointers those first few terrifying hours when you bring her home."

His thick black hair fell across his forehead in a way designed to make women desperate to push the lock back in place. Kelly was no exception. She found she had to clutch her hands together to keep from doing just that.

"Why are you doing this?" he asked.

She understood the real question. Why was she going out of her way to help a stranger—someone of whom she didn't much approve. Except by being willing to take his daughter, Tanner had forced her to look at him in a new way.

"Because I think you'll be a great dad, and I want her to have that."

Relief settled over him, easing away his tension. "Thanks, doc. I really appreciate it. I know that she's going to need a ton of stuff, but I don't have a clue where to start."

"Please, call me Kelly. And as for the baby—figuring out what to do with her can't be harder than building a hospital wing."

He grinned. "Want to bet?"

"Why don't we just wait three weeks, and you can tell me yourself."

Tanner paused outside the hospital room and thought about what he wanted to say. He knew that

Lucy wasn't going to be happy with his change of heart, but there was nothing he could do about that. He had as much right to their baby as she did. A quick call to the family lawyer his business lawyer had recommended had confirmed that.

He squared his shoulders and stepped into the room. "Hi," he said when he saw Lucy sitting up in bed.

She glanced at him for a second, gave a quick, insincere smile, then pushed the mute button on the remote and silenced the television she'd been watching.

"Tanner. I didn't expect to see you," she said, her voice flat with lack of enthusiasm. "If you're here to check up on me, I promise I'm fine. The delivery wasn't much fun, but my doctor is great. She said everything went as expected. I'll be leaving first thing in the morning. In a few weeks I'll be good as new."

"I'm glad you're all right."

He shifted uneasily and pushed his hands into his jeans pockets. He stood about five feet from the bed. The blinds were open, allowing afternoon light to spill into the room and he could see her clearly. The ordeal of giving birth had left her pale, but still beautiful. Her long, silky platinum blond hair had been pulled back into a simple braid. The high cheek bones, perfect mouth and wide green eyes were as lovely as when he'd first met her. But during their brief time together, he'd learned that she had no heart.

He couldn't help wondering what he'd seen in her all those months ago. He remembered that they'd

met at a Fourth of July picnic, and that too many
beers had caused them to end up in bed together.
He'd thought he was old enough to ignore the appeal
of a pretty face, but he'd been wrong. Or maybe
he'd just been lonely. None of that mattered now.
Whatever had first drawn them together had faded
and by the end of the weekend they were both content to part company. Until Lucy had called a couple
of months later to say she was pregnant.

She pursed her lips together. "Tanner, you're just
staring at me. You're not going to get all weird because of the baby are you?"

"Yes, but not in the way you mean."

Her gaze narrowed. Suddenly features that had
been beautiful were now merely pinched. "We've
been over this before. What exactly do you want
from me? I told you I was pregnant because I
thought it was the right thing to do. If I'd known
you were going to talk me out of having an abortion,
I wouldn't have said a word. I did as you requested—I had the kid. Now I'm giving it up for
adoption. The papers are signed. I'm not going to
change my mind."

"I am," he said quietly.

She blinked at him. "What?"

"I haven't signed the papers, and I'm not going
to. I want to keep the baby."

"Dammit, Tanner. What the hell are you thinking? If you have some fantasy about a cozy family
with me playing mommy, you can just forget it."

"I don't," he told her. "This isn't about you. As
far as you're concerned, nothing has to change. I'm
going to have a lawyer draw up some papers. Basically you walk away from the kid and I keep her.

You don't ask to see her and I don't ask for support. It's just like the adoption, only I'm going to be the one taking her."

She brushed at her smooth bangs. Her nails were long and painted a dark shade of pink. "Why don't I believe you?"

"I don't know. I'm telling the truth."

She stared at him for a long time. Tanner held his breath. He knew that Lucy couldn't stop him from keeping his daughter, but she could make things more complicated. Adoption, from her point of view, was much more tidy than the father of her child wanting to muscle in on the action.

"This isn't about you," he said. "It's about me. I don't want anything from you, except for you to sign the papers."

She continued to study him. "And if I don't, you'll haul me into court," she said, her voice resigned. "After all, I've already agreed to adoption, so I've indicated that I have no interest in my child."

"I don't know," he said honestly. "I didn't discuss that with my lawyer."

The bed had been raised so that she could sit upright but still lean against the pillows. Now she lowered the bed a few inches and closed her eyes.

"I have a great job waiting for me in L.A. I'm going to work for an agency that handles really high-powered actors, directors and producers. I'm going to be meeting these clients and entertaining them. This is my chance to move in those kind of circles." She opened her eyes and stared at him. "It's what I've always wanted. I'm beautiful enough that I'll attract the eye of some mogul type and we'll get married. I don't care if it lasts, I just want to get my foot in the door. Once I'm there, I'll make a place for myself." She sighed. "Children have never been a part of my plan. I don't want them. I don't want ours."

Her flat statement shouldn't have surprised him, but it did. He wanted to rage at her, to tell her that he'd just held the most beautiful, perfect creature in the world. How could she walk away from their tiny baby? But he didn't say a word. For one thing, Lucy wasn't going to change her mind. For another, selfishly, he wanted her gone. Lucy was many things, but maternal wasn't one of them. In this case, their daughter would be better off without her mother around to mess with her head.

"None of your plans are going to change," he said. "All I'm asking is that you sign the papers allowing me sole custody of the baby."

"Do you really think you can do this? Raise a kid on your own? What do you know about babies?"

"Less than nothing," he admitted. "But I'm willing to learn. I can't let her go, Lucy. I know that doesn't make sense to you, but I've never been more sure of anything in my life."

Her expression turned wistful. "You're a fool, Tanner Malone, but you've got a big heart. I guess that's a start."

"I can't regret her."

Lucy turned away. "I can. I guess that's the difference." She waved her left hand toward the door. "You know where I live. Have your lawyer draw up the papers and get them to me before the fifteenth. That's when I'm leaving for Los Angeles."

She looked back at him. "I don't want this kid showing up in my life in twenty years. Tell him that."

"It's a her."

"Whatever."

He nodded once. There were so many things he could have said, but why bother? He'd gotten what he'd been after. Maybe one day he would understand how someone who was so beautiful and perfect on the outside could be so incredibly ugly on the inside.

"Thanks, Lucy. My lawyer will be in touch." He turned to leave.

"Tanner?"

He paused and glanced back at her.

She flashed him her best smile, the one that had first made him saunter across the picnic area to engage her in conversation. This time all he could think of was that he couldn't wait for her to be out of his life forever.

"Thanks for the flowers."

He'd sent her a dozen roses when he'd found out she'd had the baby. He stared at the bright yellow buds, still tightly curled as if afraid to open and show themselves to the world. They were as coldly beautiful as she.

"You're welcome," he said and walked out of her room. If all went well, he would never see her again. He prayed that's what would happen.

He walked down the hallway, not really aware of his surroundings. He replayed his first meeting with Lucy a couple of times and knew that while their relationship had been a short-lived mistake, the ramifications were about to change his life forever. Because of his incredibly poor taste in women, he was about to become a father. A smile tugged at his lips. Not a bad trade.

He stopped and glanced around, then realized that he'd instinctively made his way back to the nursery. His gaze drifted over the sleeping babies, before stopping on one in particular. He already recognized that precious face. His daughter.

Panic flared in him again, along with apprehension and about fifteen other forms of "Oh, God, can I really do this?" But none of them were as strong as the sense of rightness in his heart. Maybe he was making a big mistake. Maybe he couldn't do it, but he was determined to give it all he had. They would just have to learn this whole parent-kid thing together. She was his daughter and he would die to protect her.

"Boss?"

He looked up and saw a bulldog of man standing next to him. An unlit cigar poked out from puffy lips, while eyebrows drew together in a permanently worried frown.

"What is it, Angel?" he asked.

Angel was one of three foremen in charge of the new wing. Angel's particular responsibility was coordinating the materials needed for construction.

"Toilets," Angel said glumly. He wasn't a real happy guy at the best of times. "They're wrong. We ordered fifty-six toilets and what did they send? Bidets. You know, those weird shaped things to wash your butt after—"

Tanner choked back a laugh. "I know what a bidet is. Did you call the supplier?"

"Sure, but they're squawking about how long it's

gonna take to get new ones. Then there's the light bulb problem.''

Tanner started walking toward the elevator. They had to go down to the ground floor to find their way into the construction area. Angel moved with him.

''You'd think these bozos had never heard of a light bulb before. And you won't believe what they sent me instead.''

Tanner's brain quickly focused on the problems at hand. After he'd dealt with Angel, he needed to get an update from his other foremen, then make a quick tour of the work completed in the past couple of days. After that, he had reports and a meeting with his bookkeeper about who had been paid what. Then he was meeting Kelly Hall at six. Hell, it was never going to get done.

But instead of being discouraged, he found himself continuing to smile. Because it wasn't every day that a man became a father.

Kelly tapped her pen impatiently against her desk. Be there, she willed silently, waiting for her friend to pick up the phone. While she waited, she glanced up at the clock. Her afternoon appointments started in ten minutes, which meant if Ronni didn't pick up soon, they weren't going to be able to talk until that evening. Kelly figured she disrupted her patients' lives enough by having to cancel without warning if there was a baby to deliver, that the least she could do was be on time when she was in the office.

''Dr. Powers,'' a familiar voice said crisply.

Kelly sighed in relief. ''It's Kelly and I did a really stupid thing.''

Ronni Powers, a pediatrician and close friend for

the past three years, laughed. "No way your stupid thing can top my stupid thing. I had sex without a condom and got pregnant. Now how are you going to beat that?"

Kelly smiled. "Don't give me that. You're thrilled about the baby."

"Thrilled, but still in shock. Besides, I'm supposed to be a responsible adult. No one is going to believe me if I don't act like one."

"You do, most of the time." She paused and tried to figure out the best way to ask her question. "I need you to tell me if Tanner Malone is a good man."

"That's your stupid thing?"

"Sort of. Did you know about his baby?"

"Sure," Ronni said. "Ryan told me. Tanner was involved with some woman over the summer. The relationship didn't work out but she ended up pregnant. She was due any time now, wasn't she?"

"She had the baby today," Kelly said.

"I didn't know that. Well, as I understand it, both she and Tanner had agreed to give up the child for adoption. Is there a problem?"

"That depends on whether or not Tanner is a decent guy. He changed his mind. He's keeping his daughter."

This time Ronni was the one who got quiet. Kelly pictured her green eyes widening with shock as her mouth dropped open.

"Tanner's keeping the baby?"

"That's the plan. As far as I know Lucy will still be giving her up, so Tanner's going to have sole custody. Do you think he can manage?" Kelly rubbed her temple. "I feel a little responsible. I'm the one who dragged him to the nursery so he could hold her. You know what it's like to cradle a newborn.''

''Pretty amazing,'' Ronni agreed. ''I'm stunned by the news. Fortunately, Tanner seems to be a great guy. He's wonderful with Ryan's kids, but being an uncle is very different than being a father.''

''That's what I think,'' Kelly agreed. ''I know that there are a lot of single parents, but most of them have some kind of warning. Tanner made his decision today and the baby goes home tomorrow. Not much time to prepare.''

''You're right,'' Ronni said. ''He can't even take a couple of weeks off because of the construction project at the hospital. He's been working too many hours as it is, just to get things caught up. What was he thinking?''

''So you think I was wrong to encourage him?''

''Not for a minute,'' Ronni told her. ''All this stuff is just logistics, Kelly. How can it be wrong for a man to love his child? And don't give me any lines about mothers being more nurturing. I don't believe that and I don't think you do, either.''

''No, I don't.'' How could she? Her mother had died shortly after she'd been born and her father had raised her on his own. In her opinion, he'd done a wonderful job. She couldn't imagine a parent being more supportive or caring.

''So it's just a matter of getting Tanner up to speed,'' Ronni said. Kelly heard her flipping pages in her date book, then her friend continued. ''I'm free tomorrow. I'll check with Ryan and see if we can go over and help him. Maybe a couple of lessons with a doll will prepare him for that first diaper change.''

The thought of Tanner Malone bent over staring at the contents of a newborn's diaper made Kelly smile. "He's not going to like that part at all."

"Few people do."

Kelly cleared her throat. "Yes, well, I'm going to help out, too. I figure it's the least I could do after getting him in this mess."

"You're not the one who had the baby."

Kelly could feel her cheeks getting hot, which was silly. She pressed the back of her free hand against her skin. "I know, but, well, anyway, I'm meeting him tonight. We're going to a baby store and I'm going to help him pick out furniture. I also thought I'd take him one of those books on what happens during the first year."

"Dr. Hall, do you sound flustered?"

"Of course not. I'm just watching the clock. I have patients in a couple of minutes."

"I think not. I think you are, in fact, interested in Tanner."

"You're crazy. I'm helping out a friend."

"Oh. When did you two become friends?"

Kelly glared at the phone. "Fine. I'm helping a fellow human being in need."

"You're hiding the truth, maybe even from yourself. I think *you* think he's hot."

"I'm concerned about a new father taking care of a child when he's had no preparation or experience. My thoughts are for the baby, not Tanner."

Ronni sighed. "All right. Have it your way, but you're missing out. I have to tell you, there's something pretty wonderful about those Malone brothers.''

Kelly smiled. Ronni was marrying Ryan Malone at the end of the month. "I think you've been influenced by your relationship with Ryan."

"Maybe, but only in the best way possible. Besides, would it kill you to be interested in a man? You've been living like a nun for the past three years."

"Sure. I always take relationship advice from a woman in the middle of an unplanned pregnancy."

Ronni laughed. "Oh, thanks. Throw that in my face. But think about what I said. It would be very sad for you to ignore this opportunity."

"Say good-bye, Ronni."

"Bye."

Kelly was still smiling when she hung up the phone. She collected her charts and made her way out of her office, all the while ignoring the little voice that whispered Ronni might be on to something after all.

Chapter Three

Kelly glanced at her watch. Four minutes after six. Not bad, considering she'd stopped at a local bookstore to pick up something for Tanner. She pushed through the swinging doors that separated the hospital from the new wing still under construction. From there, she passed through an alcove and hanging sheets of plastic, then found herself in the middle of a beehive.

Despite the fact that for much of the city the workday had ended, dozens of construction personnel labored on. She could see the framing that in time would be the new pediatric floor. To her right was the lab set-up, still little more than an outline of a room. The only remotely finished section of the first floor was the new daycare center, probably because it would be opening first.

She turned right. Tanner had left her a voice mail

that afternoon telling her that she could find him in his office, which was in what would eventually be the new lab. As she crossed the plywood floor, she saw a big sign warning that this was a hard hat area, then saw a stack of the yellow construction headgear on a table below the banner.

Kelly picked one up and plopped it on her head, all the while trying not to think about the last dozen or so people who had done the same. Then she made her way in the general direction of Tanner's office.

It wasn't hard to find. Signs spray-painted directly onto the unfinished walls pointed the way to various locations on the construction site. "Boss-man's office" was marked in red with a ten foot long arrow. She followed it to the end and found herself entering a medium sized room with a desk, several chairs and building plans covering most of the walls.

Tanner sat behind the desk, staring at lists and making notes. The overhead lighting was harsh but he still looked as handsome as she remembered. His brother, Ryan, was also a good-looking guy. Talk about a great gene pool. Between her father's roguish appeal and her mother's model-perfect beauty, Baby Ames—make that Baby Malone—was going to be a looker herself.

Kelly leaned against the door frame and studied Tanner. He was lost in his work and hadn't noticed her presence. She thought about all he was going to have to deal with over the next few weeks as he adjusted to life with a newborn. If nothing else, it would be a great test of his character. She just hoped he was up to it.

"Ready to go shopping?" she asked.

He raised his head, then smiled when he saw her.

That same smile that made her feel sixteen and awkward. It also did funny things to her stomach and her knees, which she didn't remember from high school. Oh, Tanner Malone was a deadly combination of male beauty and charm, but she was fairly immune. At thirty-two, no man had really captured her attention and there was no reason to think anyone was going to do that now.

"Kelly," he said, his voice pleased. "Thanks for meeting me here. I had some paperwork to finish up."

"It wasn't a problem. I had something I wanted to get before we went shopping anyway."

His gaze dropped to the bag she carried. "Generally I like unexpected presents, but this time I'm not so sure."

"Don't be scared. It's not going to bite you." She set the package on his desk, then waited while he pulled out the book.

"*What To Expect The First Year,*" he read. "It's really thick."

"Yes, but there are a lot of pictures and a ton of valuable information. Everything you'll need to know to survive those first twelve months." She pointed to a slip of paper sticking out the top of the book. "I've marked the pages that talk about buying for a baby."

Tanner opened the book. His expression shifted quickly from stunned surprise to amazement to shock. "This list is longer than all the material requisitions for the entire hospital wing."

She grinned. "Not quite. But babies need a lot of stuff. How's the balance on your credit card?"

He flipped the pages, shaking his head slowly.

"They're all fine. I pay them off each month and they have big limits."

"Oh, good. You're going to be needing that."

"I can tell."

He rose to his feet and grabbed his jacket and a hard hat from two nails sticking out of the wall, then took the book. "I guess we'd better get started." He looked shell-shocked.

"Are you all right?"

"Yeah. I'm just trying not to think about it too much. If I let myself dwell on the fact that this time tomorrow I'm going to have a baby in my house, I might be tempted to head for the hills."

"You'll be fine. Just take things one step at a time."

"Easy for you to say. You're a doctor." He followed her back to the entrance, where they both dropped off their hats. "I guess we should take my car," he said as they walked through the hospital. "I drive an Explorer, so there will be plenty of space for furniture."

"Good idea." She didn't dare tell him that she doubted they would fit everything in his sports utility vehicle in just one trip.

Tanner shrugged into his jacket, then held the door open for her. He was parked in the main parking lot, which had been recently enlarged as part of the new project.

"I appreciate you helping me with this," he said, leading the way to a black Explorer. "I'm sure you're very busy and it's nice of you to give up your time."

"I'm glad to help," she said sincerely. "Most parents have several months to get used to the idea of having a baby around. They take classes, talk to other parents, buy slowly. You're going from zero to sixty in less than twenty-four hours. It's a daunting concept.''

He flashed her a grin. ''So you're trying to tell me that it's okay to be terrified?''

''You wouldn't be normal if you weren't. But I have every confidence in you.'' Which she did, she thought with some surprise as he unlocked the passenger door and held it open for her.

She stepped up into the well-used, but clean vehicle. Her skirt rode up slightly on her leg and she had to resist the urge to cover her thighs with her hands. Like Tanner was even looking, she thought.

Even as she tried to casually glance at him, he was closing the door and heading to the driver's side. So much for bowling him over with her feminine charms, she thought humorously. So what if the man made her body react in ways it hadn't before. All that meant was that she wasn't dead. She should enjoy the occasional flickers and sparks. Feeling them didn't mean she had to do anything about them.

He backed out of the space, then drove toward the exit. ''Which way?''

''Do you know the big electronics store on the corner of Green's Way and Carson?''

''Sure.''

''There's a place called Baby Town in the same shopping center.''

He glanced at her and frowned. ''Are you sure? I've never noticed it.''

''I'm not surprised. We only see what's important to us at the time. You probably never noticed the designer outlet beside the electronics store, while I didn't know there was a sporting goods store there until I called for directions and they told me the baby store was next to it.''

''Gotcha,'' he said, then concentrated on his driving.

Kelly leaned back in the seat and tried not to stare at her companion. Why was he so intriguing? Was it because he was about to take on a daunting task? Or was it more simple—had she just gotten tired of being on her own? She couldn't remember her last date. Certainly she hadn't been out with a man since she'd moved to Honeygrove and that was three years ago. Talk about pathetic.

''I talked to Ronni today,'' Tanner said, interrupting her thoughts. ''She said you'd called her.''

Kelly pressed her lips together, not sure if she should apologize for that. Before she could decide, Tanner continued.

''I appreciate that you wanted to check me out. I'm an unknown to you, some construction worker who suddenly wants to keep his kid. You're concerned about the baby's welfare. Thanks for that.''

''You're welcome. I'm glad you understand why I did it.''

''Sure. You want to make sure I'm decent father material.'' His mouth twisted down. ''I don't know what the hell I'm doing, but I'll give it my best shot. Of course Ronni didn't help things.''

''What do you mean?'' She couldn't imagine her friend being difficult.

''The good news is that she said she would be happy to be the baby's pediatrician. That's a relief. I mean Ronni's going to be in the family and everything. Once she marries Ryan at the end of the month, I'll even know how to get her at home." He grinned, then the smile faded. "It was the rest of what she said that scared me. She says she knows a couple of great baby nurses. Aren't babies too small to need their own nurse?"

"It's because they are small they have a nurse."

"Yeah, well, that's what Ronni said. She pointed out what we already talked about—that I can't put her in day care for a while and that I have to be at work, so a baby nurse is a good solution. In a few weeks I can look into home day care until she's old enough for a regular place. I've even been thinking of getting a college kid or someone like that to look after her at my office. Not the one at the hospital," he said. "I meant after the project's done. There's room and I'd see her more."

Kelly impulsively touched Tanner's arm. "I know it seems overwhelming right now, but you're taking things one step at a time. That's what's important. The baby nurse is a great idea. It will give you some space to make other decisions. As for bringing your child to work—I think it's terrific that you want to."

"Yeah?" He looked at her briefly, before returning his attention to the road. "I guess. Ryan told me that Lily said she'd be available in a pinch. Lily is Ryan's mother-in-law." He frowned. "Is that right? Her daughter was Ryan's first wife. When Patricia died, Lily moved in to help with the kids. She's still there and plans to stay. Anyway, she said she's happy to help out, but I figure she's got her hands full with Ryan's three. Plus Ronni's pregnant, so that's going to make four kids."

He pulled into the parking lot. "I wish I could

take time off work, but with the hospital wing still behind schedule, it's not possible.'' He stomped on the brakes and swore under his breath. ''I've never seen that before. And it's huge.''

Kelly glanced out the window and saw the Baby Town store. Pastel blocks, the size of trucks, stood above the entrance. Teddy bears and rabbits tumbled and marched across the painted windows.

After parking the car, he stopped the engine, but didn't get out right away. ''I spoke to Lucy,'' he said. ''She's going to sign off on the kid. She doesn't want to be involved. I know the relationship was a mistake, but I'm kind of surprised she's just going to walk away. It's not that she *can* do it so much as it seems like it's going to be easy for her.''

Kelly didn't know what to say to that. After all, she'd given up a child, too. But for her, it had been anything but easy. In fact the pain continued to haunt her, fifteen years after the fact. ''Not every woman finds it easy to walk away.''

''Probably,'' he agreed. He looked at her. ''Listen to me. This is the most I've talked in a month. I'm sorry for dumping it all on you.''

''Tanner, don't apologize,'' she told him. ''Really. I'm happy to listen. You're working through a lot, and in my opinion, you're incredibly calm.''

''That's on the outside.''

''In time you'll be calm on the inside, too. You and your daughter will get used to each other. You'll develop a relationship with rituals that will be so meaningful, you won't be able to imagine what life was like without her. I'm happy to be a part of this.''

''I have this bad feeling that the only reason I'm

going forward with this is that I don't have a clue as to how hard it's going to be.''

Kelly couldn't help laughing. ''Unfortunately, you're exactly right.''

This was hell, Tanner thought grimly from his place in the center of the store. Hell with miniature furniture and too many cutesy, fuzzy things. He looked around and spotted Kelly talking to one of the salespeople. The older woman was nodding and typing information into a computer.

Not knowing what else to do, he glanced at a display of quilts. They were small, about four feet by three feet. He turned over the price tag and took a step back. Six hundred dollars? He peered at the quilt again, trying to figure out why on earth it cost so much. Jeez. Six hundred dollars. He thought about the list in the book and swallowed hard. Kelly hadn't been kidding about his credit limit. He wondered if it was going to be enough.

''Okay, here's the plan,'' Kelly said, coming to stand next to him. ''I had the store— What's wrong? You're practically green.''

He pointed to the quilt. ''It's six hundred dollars. If a scrap of cloth costs that, how much is a crib?''

She looked from him to the quilt, then fingered the cream colored lace and read the tag. When she returned her attention to him, humor danced in her hazel brown eyes. ''Don't panic, big boy. That's a handmade quilt, covered with imported lace. They're a one of a kind item, and not for the likes of us.''

He breathed a sigh of relief.

''Besides,'' she added casually, ''babies spit up

on just about everything, so it's better to have bedding you can just throw in the washer."

Her words planted an image in Tanner's brain that made him uncomfortable. "How much do they spit up?"

"Don't worry about that now," Kelly said. She waved a long computer printout in front of him. "This is a basic baby registry. It lists every possible item a baby could use. Between that and the list in the book, we'll be sure to remember the important stuff. This second list tells us what's in stock. There's no point in falling in love with a crib or dresser only to find out it's not available."

"I don't generally fall for furniture," Tanner muttered, but Kelly wasn't listening.

"Let's start with the big stuff," she said. "Crib, stroller, car seat, changing table, dresser, maybe a couple of mobiles. Then we'll move onto linens, bath stuff and clothes." She tapped the list. "You'll want some kind of portable crib, as well, so you can take her to a baby-sitter, or even to work. They have some that turn into playpens for when they're older."

Tanner could only nod as he tried to take in what she was saying. He felt as if he'd entered a strange and frightening new world and he wondered if it was too late to go back.

"Furniture," Kelly said, pointing to the large display on the far side of the store.

He followed her down an aisle crammed with car seats and wondered how on earth he was going to pick one. Maybe he should have asked Ryan to come along. He knew about this kind of stuff. But it hadn't occurred to Tanner that buying a kid a bed or a car seat was going to be complicated.

"How big is the room?" Kelly asked. "And is there furniture in there now? Do we have to work around anything?"

Tanner shook his head. "I have a guest room, but it's not furnished. It's about twelve by fourteen, with a big closet."

"Okay, so size isn't an issue. Basically all cribs serve the same function. These are all new and look well-made. The important factors are the height of the mattress when it's all the way up, and the spacing of the rails. So pick what you like and then we'll check for the safety features. I'm guessing all of them are going to comply with safety recommendations."

Pick what he liked? He looked at the various displays. Many were set up to look like individual rooms. There were dividers covered with wallpaper and border prints, cribs filled with ruffled comforters and too many stuffed animals for any man to be comfortable. He found himself stepping around fuzzy bears and pink elephants. There were tigers and lions, fluffy kittens, puppies and some creatures of undetermined species.

He glanced from the displays to Kelly and back. The cribs all looked the same to him. Too-small beds with guard rails. The dressers were almost normal looking.

"What kind of wood do you like?" Kelly asked, coming to his rescue. "Light or dark. Or would you prefer something painted?"

She stood next to him, looking patient and completely comfortable. Was this a chick thing? Did all women have the baby gene, or was she relaxed because part of her job was bringing infants into the world?

He allowed himself a moment to appreciate the way the overhead lights played on her medium blond hair. It fell to about the middle of her back and she'd pulled it into a neat, but fancy braid. Bangs hung down to her eyebrows, but in a soft, sexy way that made him think about wanting—

Down boy, he told himself. He didn't have time to get distracted. His life was one big crisis right now and he didn't have room to add attraction to a female doctor to his list.

"I don't know what she'd like," he said. "You used to be a little girl. What would have made you happy?"

"I'm not sure babies have strong opinions on furniture, but I'll give it a try." Kelly turned in a circle, then pointed to a display of white furniture.

They moved to that aisle. While Kelly read the tag and made sure the rails were the right distance apart—or whatever—he checked the construction, the quality of wood used and made sure there were no sharp edges.

"I like it," she said. "What do you think?"

He shrugged. He wouldn't have picked white as his first choice, but then his first choice wasn't being here, either. "It's fine."

But she wasn't listening. Instead her face had taken on an expression of such tenderness, Tanner felt his blood heat up about ten degrees. Then he noticed that her longing gaze wasn't directed at him, but instead focused on a comforter in the next display. He stared at it, blinked twice and bit back a groan.

If he'd given a second's thought to decorating a child's room, he would have pictured primary colors, or building blocks, or maybe even a train. But that's not what had caught Kelly's eye. She'd been transfixed by a pink-and-white comforter decorated with a teddy bear in a ballerina get-up.

"It's darling," she said, taking his sleeve and tugging. "Don't you love it?" She pulled him toward the display. "They have the comforter and linens and bumper pads. Oh, look, there's a diaper stacker. I'll bet there's a border print for the walls and even a valance for the window. You could…"

Her voice trailed off. She released his sleeve and nodded. "You hate it."

Hate implied an emotional energy he wasn't willing to commit to ballerina teddy bears. Kelly was a woman. She'd once been a little girl. Therefore her taste had to be better than his. With any luck, the pattern would fade in the wash.

"It's fine," he said. "Let's get it. What's next on the list?"

"But Tanner, you don't think it's cute. We can pick something else."

He looked at her and found himself intrigued by her height. In her heels, she was only about an inch shorter than him. He'd generally gone in for the petite types, but there was something to be said for looking a woman dead in the eye without having to tilt his head.

"Kelly, this is fine. I'm sure she'll adore it."

By this time, the sales clerk had joined them. She was a middle-aged woman with a cheerful smile. By the way she kept out of the discussion Tanner suspected she'd heard more then her share of arguments over baby accessories.

"If you're sure," Kelly said, and turned to her. "All right. The white crib, the four-drawer dresser, and the three-drawer changing table. Then this bedding set with the diaper stacker." She paused. "We can worry about the wallpaper another time."

Like never, he thought, trying *not* to picture a wall covered with ballerina teddy bears. The three of them moved on.

They spent nearly thirty minutes in a discussion about car seats before they all agreed on one. Then they chose a mattress, crib pads, receiving blankets—although he didn't know what they were going to receive—towels with hoods, a stroller and dozens of things he couldn't recognize. Tanner surprised them and himself by insisting on a mobile of fuzzy animals, of which his favorite was the lion, and a matching wall hanging.

When they moved onto baby clothing, he told himself not to watch as Kelly chose tiny shirts and nighties and wrap, sleeper things with and without feet. The store clerk carried armloads over to the cash register, then returned for more. They even bought a diaper bag, which Tanner could not imagine having to carry through the construction site. When they reached the stage of discussing bottles for feeding and the best brand of diapers, he couldn't stand it anymore. He touched Kelly's arm.

"Could I talk to you for a minute?" he asked.

"Sure." She excused them from the clerk and led him to a corner of the store. "What's wrong?"

"I can't do this," he said. "You're buying bottles

and I don't know how to physically feed her. Or how much. Or how warm it's supposed to be.'' He could hear the sharp edge to his voice, but didn't think he could control it.

Kelly looked at him for a long time, then reached in her purse for her cell phone. Tanner panicked. Was she calling the hospital to tell them he couldn't be trusted with his own child?

''Ronni, hi, it's me. I'm with Tanner at the baby store.'' She paused, then smiled. ''Oh, he's definitely having a dose of reality and he's looking longingly at the door. But he'll be fine. Tomorrow, when you drop by Tanner's to give him the diaper changing lesson, could you also teach him about feeding and anything else he might need? You know, the first-time parent baby lesson.'' She paused again, then smiled. ''Clueless is a strong term, but in this case appropriate. I'll let him know. Thanks. Bye.''

She hung up. ''That was your sister-in-law to-be.''

''I guessed that.'' He was going to complain that he wasn't clueless, but unfortunately he was. It was pretty sad.

''Ronni's going to phone the hospital and arrange for them to keep Baby Malone until early afternoon. Ronni and Ryan will come over to your place in the morning. Ryan will help with whatever furniture isn't finished and Ronni will take you through the basics.''

Some of the tension in his chest eased. ''That's great.''

''And as I already promised, I'm available this weekend.'' She pointed to the impressive pile by the cash register. ''All that isn't going to fit in your car.

I suggest we take home as much as we can, starting with the biggest things. I'll swing by tomorrow and get the rest of it.''

He didn't know what to say to her. Part of him wanted to explain that while her offer was really nice, he didn't want to put her out. But that was a very small part of his brain. The rest was doing a cheer in relief.

"Thanks," he said. "I don't want to think about spending that first afternoon with her by myself.''

"You won't.''

He studied her face. She was pretty enough, but not a beauty. Not at all the normal kind of woman who caught his eye. "Why are you doing this?" he asked.

"Because I want to," she said easily. "I think you and your daughter deserve a fighting chance and I want to give you that.''

"Thanks," he told her, and had the sudden urge to give her a hug.

That would be dumb, he reminded himself. Dr. Kelly Hall wasn't interested in him—she was concerned about the baby. As long as he remembered that, they would both be fine.

Chapter Four

It was a few minutes after eight the next morning when Kelly knocked on Tanner's front door. She juggled to keep the two large coffees from spilling as she balanced the bag of bagels and cream cheese. She figured Tanner wouldn't have thought to eat much in the past twenty-four hours. Certainly neither of them had eaten dinner the night before.

She heard footsteps from inside the two story house, then he opened the door.

"Morning," he said.

Kelly could barely manage a squeak in response. He'd obviously been up most of the night. There were dark shadows under his eyes and his expression was slightly dazed. But he'd showered that morning. His strong jaw was freshly shaved and the dampness in his hair only added sheen where the light reflected on the thick dark layers.

His clothing wasn't all that much different than it had been the day before. A soft-looking, worn sweatshirt replaced the long sleeved shirt he'd had on the previous day, but he still wore jeans and boots, although today the latter were cowboy, instead of reinforced work boots.

"Morning," she managed on her second attempt to speak. "You look tired. Did you sleep at all?"

He shrugged. Big, muscled shoulders made a casual male movement. It shouldn't have affected her heart rate, but it did. Her palms got a little damp, too, and she had to worry about the coffee slipping and falling.

"A couple of hours. Mostly I just worked and worried." He motioned for her to come into the house.

"You'll be fine," she said, handing him a cup of coffee as she entered. "It's not as if you're going to be on your own. Ronni is going to come by and give you that lesson in basic baby care and I'll be right here." She smiled. "Although I do have to warn you I have a couple of patients ready to go into labor. I'm caught in one of those cycles. Currently over two-thirds of my practice is in various stages of pregnancy. I have twelve due in the next four weeks, if you can believe it."

He glanced at the pager she'd clipped to the waistband of her jeans. Some of the worry left his eyes. "I have one of those too, but when it goes off, it's just a building crisis. Not one about giving birth."

"Such are the differences in our professions." She handed him the bag. "Bagels. Did you eat last night?"

He shook his head.

"I figured you wouldn't. Men get upset and they stop eating. Most women go in the other direction. I know during finals there were semesters when I felt like I was chowing my way through the entire candy aisle of the student union."

His gaze brushed over her body before returning to her face. "You'd never know it."

"That's because I'm tall." After a moment of relaxing, she found herself getting nervous again. It was all this body talk. She didn't know how to handle it. For as long as she could remember, her body had been merely functional. She didn't think of herself as especially feminine and certainly not sexy. But around Tanner, she remembered she was a woman and she enjoyed the fact.

"I spoke to the hospital this morning," she said briskly, to change the subject. "Your daughter had a great night. She's sleeping well, taking formula with no problem and she'll be released any time after noon. You just have to go pick her up."

"Okay," he said cautiously.

"Don't worry. Ronni will be here in about an hour and she'll take you over all you need to know. At the hospital, one of the nurses will give you the same lesson, so you'll have reinforcement. Besides, I'll be here through the weekend."

"Yeah, okay," he muttered, but he didn't sound convinced. He shifted awkwardly. "I put together most of the baby furniture and some of the clothes."

"I'd love to see what you've done," she said. "And when we're finished, we can empty my car. It's packed."

The previous evening she and Tanner had loaded

as much as possible into his Explorer, then he'd taken Kelly back to the hospital. There, she'd collected her own car, returned to the store and taken the rest of their purchases, which she was delivering this morning. Tanner had looked stunned by the amount they had bought, so she hadn't had the heart to tell him there was a lot more yet to buy. She figured she would make the grocery-drug store run later that afternoon to stock up on lotions, shampoo, baby wipes, a thermometer and the like.

Tanner took a couple of steps into the house, then paused. ''Want the nickel tour of the place?'' he asked.

''I'd love it.'' She glanced around at the spacious living room. There wasn't any furniture yet, but the walls had been stripped of wallpaper and she could see that he was in the middle of refinishing the wood around the bay windows. Underneath the drop cloths on the floor, she spotted scarred but still beautiful hardwood.

''I'm working on this room now,'' he said. ''I've been doing a room at a time, mostly because that's all I have time for. Sometimes I think I should just get a crew in here and finish it, but I like doing the work myself. It's relaxing.''

He led the way down a short hall. To her left she saw a dining room. The walls were still covered with a flocked print in burgundy and gold. Heavy furniture made the large space seem small and dark.

''I bought that set from the former owners of the house. It's about a hundred years old. It's in great shape. When I finish a few more rooms, I'm going to start moving pieces around. The table and buffet can stay in the dining room, but I'll move the old armoire into the guest room."

"But you're keeping the wallpaper, right? I mean it's so you."

He opened his mouth, then closed it. A grin tugged at the corners. "You had me going there for a second. I thought you really liked it."

"Scary, huh? Someone must have liked it. Not only is it in this dining room, but I'm willing to bet it wasn't ordered custom, which means hundreds of people chose it."

"You wouldn't believe some of the ugly stuff I've seen in houses I've remodeled." He continued down the short hall, which ended in a bright, open kitchen. "Before I bought the company, they were split about fifty-fifty between residential and commercial contracting. I changed that, making the business one hundred percent commercial. I'd rather work on one big job for four or five months than have sixteen small ones."

He set the bagels on the counter and took a sip of his coffee. "The kitchen turned out pretty good."

She turned in a slow circle, taking in the beautifully fitted and finished cabinets, the granite countertops and a large stove that would make any cook weep with joy. "Did you do the cabinets yourself?"

"Yeah. I made them up because it was more fun than ordering them. It took about a year, but I didn't mind."

To the right of the kitchen was an oversized family room. There were two sofas and a couple of recliners, along with a movie-theater sized television and more remote controls than she'd ever seen outside of an electronics store. He caught her studying the coffee table and smiled sheepishly.

"Okay, I know. I'm a guy. What can I say? I like my toys."

"I guess."

Sliding doors on the far side of the room led to a huge backyard complete with room for a play area.

"This is very nice," she told him. "You have a beautiful home."

"Thanks. The baby's room is upstairs. I'm converting the guest room because that's where I started remodeling. I needed a small project to make sure I remembered everything," he said as he led the way up the stairs. "Owning the company has meant spending more time in the office and less time working on the projects."

At the top of the stairs, around to the left, were a pair of double doors leading to the master suite. Kelly caught a quick glimpse of a king-sized bed, a sitting area complete with fireplace and beyond that, a bathroom to die for. Then Tanner was motioning her across the hall.

The new baby's room was large with cream colored walls and a bay seat window. Tanner had put together the four-drawer dresser and the crib. The three-drawer changing table was still in pieces, but he'd put the rocking chair into the alcove by the closet and moved in a floor lamp. A couple of bags of bedding and clothes reminded her that she still had a car full of stuff downstairs, but before she could mention that, her gaze fell on the mobile hanging over the crib.

She crossed the thickly carpeted floor and turned the key activating the mobile. Instantly music filled

the room and the collection of fuzzy animals began
to turn in a slow circle. Of all the items in the room,
this was the one that made her realize that Tanner
Malone was really going to have a baby in his life.
Waiting in the hospital was his own precious child.

So many years had gone by since she'd given up
her daughter for adoption. For the most part, the
pain of loss had dulled. While she frequently
thought about her daughter, she didn't ache for her
very much anymore. Unless something happened—
something like seeing someone else have the very
thing she'd given away.

"What are you thinking?" he asked.

"That you're very lucky. You have a lovely
daughter." She gave him a quick smile. "Sorry. I
don't mean to get emotional, it's just that I always
wanted a large family and it doesn't look like that's
going to happen."

He leaned against the door frame and folded his
arms over his chest. "Why hasn't it? You could
have an even dozen by now."

That made her laugh. "I wasn't looking for *that*
many." She paused. "I'm not sure of the reason.
Some of it is being a doctor. Medical school, then
my residency didn't leave much time for a personal
life."

"So what's your excuse now?"

What was her excuse? She couldn't tell him the
truth…that her past made her feel guilty and small.
That if any man knew about the flaws in her character, he would never want her. She knew that her
sense of lacking worthiness was something she
should work on, but she'd never found the time.
Somehow it was always easier to get lost in her job.

"I'm not sure I have an excuse," she told him. "It takes time to get established in a new town. I haven't met anyone who interests me. You know, the usual stuff."

He grimaced. "That makes sense. I, on the other hand, have had too many relationships, but that's going to change now."

She couldn't hold back her smile. "Don't be so fast to think so. Many women will find you even more attractive now that you have a child."

"It's not about them," he said. "It's about me. For the past few months, I've been looking at my life and I'm not sure I like what I see. It was one thing to fool around while I was on my own, but now I have a child to think about. She deserves a father who makes good relationship choices. I want her to be proud of me."

Kelly couldn't help thinking that Tanner was much deeper than she would have given him credit for. Between the muscles, the incredibly blue eyes and the smile that screamed seduction, she would have thought him to be a player, with no interest in anything of value. And she would have been wrong.

The doorbell rang.

"I bet that's Ronni. She probably brought Ryan along," he said as he headed for the stairs.

Kelly followed him. Ronni and Ryan stood in the family room. Ryan held up a container holding three cups of coffee, and a pink box from a bakery. "I see we both thought to bring breakfast," he said with a smile. "Great minds think alike."

"Good to see you both," Kelly said. "I brought bagels."

Ronni set down the brightly wrapped gift box

she'd been holding and reached for the bag of bagels. "Thank you, Kelly. I'm dying for a danish, but I can't eat all that sugar on an empty stomach. It makes me queasy. So I'll have a bagel first. Then a danish. Maybe even two."

She glanced up and saw everyone staring at her. "What?" she asked, sounding indignant. "I'm eating for two."

Kelly shook her head. "Fine. Eat for two. But don't be screaming when you step on the scale for your monthly appointment."

Ronni pressed her lips together. "Fine. I'll have half a bagel and then half a danish." She sighed. "I never knew I'd hate having one of my friends also be my doctor."

Tanner looked startled by the exchange. "Are all women like this when they're pregnant? Maybe it was a good thing that Lucy and I weren't really spending time together."

Ryan hugged Ronni and brushed his cheek against her red hair. "Pregnancy is full of challenges, but the end results are worth it. Besides, Ronni is an angel."

Ronni shook her head. "He's humoring me because he thinks if he keeps sweet-talking me, I won't throw up later today. My morning sickness tends to hit more mid-afternoon. It's really fun during office hours." She shoved the box toward Tanner then reached for the bag of bagels. "Open this, Dad."

Tanner stared at the box. "It's for me?"

"No, it's for your daughter."

"Oh. Thanks." He sounded more confused than sincere, then he reached for the box and studied the paper.

It showed pink angels and curly mauve hearts. Tied on top was a small pink rattle. Looking more uncomfortable by the second, he ripped into the paper, then lifted the lid off the square box.

First he pulled out a frilly dress in pale peach. The tiny sleeves had little bows and there was lace on the hem.

"It's beautiful," Kelly said. "Ronni, that's so adorable."

"I know. I fell in love with it the second I saw it. I adore Drew and Griffin," she said, naming Ryan's two boys, "but shopping for them is not as much fun as shopping for their sister. All those lacy, frilly whatevers. It's great."

"It's a dress," Tanner said doubtfully. "Does she need a dress?"

"All girls do," Ronni said as she cut a bagel in half and smoothed on cream cheese. "For when you take her out."

"Take her out where?"

"Anywhere. Don't you want her to look good?"

Tanner stared at the dress as if it were a subversive plot to overthrow the government. Kelly was worried he might bolt at any moment.

"What else is in there?" she asked to distract him.

"There's more?" Tanner sounded more alarmed than pleased.

Kelly noticed that Ryan wasn't saying much, but he appeared to be highly amused by his brother's apprehension. She studied the two Malone brothers noting the similarities in their dark hair and blue eyes. Ryan was a little taller and more slender, while Tanner was solid muscle.

"Well, this is okay, I guess," Tanner said, holding up a stuffed bear. Then he glanced at a book touting the joys of having a daughter. "I'll need this for sure. I've finally figured out I don't know diddly about women."

"Fortunately she's not going to be a woman for a long time," Kelly said. "You will have learned a lot by then."

"Which reminds me," Ronni said as she licked cream cheese off her fingers. "I brought my practice baby. She's in the car, along with diapers and bath stuff."

"I'll get it," Ryan said.

"I'll come with you," Kelly told him. "My car is filled with the things Tanner couldn't bring home last night."

"Then we'll all make the trip outside," Tanner said as he set the gifts on the kitchen counter.

Ronni waved. "You go ahead. I just want to eat more."

Kelly was still laughing when her pager beeped. She glanced at the display and recognized the number for the hospital. The code following told her that she had a patient in labor.

"I'll be right with you," she said as she drew the mobile phone out of her purse. Two minutes later she'd confirmed that one of her pregnant patients intended to give birth later that morning.

"I have to run," she told Tanner as she walked out toward her car. He'd unloaded most of the bags she'd picked up from the store and was holding an overnight bag. "You might as well take that inside."

"So you'll be back?"

She tried not to smile at the panic in his voice. "I promised I'd stay, and I will. I don't expect this to take too long, so look for me later this afternoon. When are you picking up the baby?"

"Around eleven," he said. He swallowed. "So you'll really be back?"

She touched his arm. Through the soft, worn sweatshirt, she felt the firmness of his muscles. She squeezed. "Don't worry. You'll be fine. Ryan and Ronni are here. She'll give you your baby lesson and that will give you the confidence you need to handle this. Remember when you first started working for the construction company? Didn't you have a lot of things to learn?"

He nodded. "But if I screwed up I wasn't messing up a kid."

"You're not going to mess her up. In fact, I'm willing to bet you're really going to like being a father."

"Yeah?"

She released him. "I promise. See you later."

With that she got in her car and started the engine. As she backed down the driveway, she couldn't suppress a faint thrill of excitement that she was going to be coming back later. She wanted to spend more time with Tanner. She told herself it was because of the baby and nothing else, but she wasn't sure that she really believed that. In her heart of hearts, she knew that somehow it had become something more.

"Okay, I know you're worried," Tanner said as he carefully steered his Explorer onto the main road. He had to force himself to merge with traffic when all he wanted to do was drive twenty in the slow lane so he could be sure they got home safely.

At the stoplight, he quickly glanced over his shoulder and saw his daughter sleeping soundly in her car seat. Hope and love and terror battled it out in his chest. He felt like he'd been sucker punched and handed his heart's desire, all in the same moment. Nothing was ever going to be the same again.

"We'll get through this," he told her, then returned his attention to the road. "I've screwed up more than once in my life, but I swear, I'll do my damnedest not to screw up with you." He paused, then cleared his throat. "I should probably start by not swearing in front of you, huh? Sorry about that. See I don't have any practice at being a father. Fortunately you don't have any practice at being a kid, either. So we'll learn together. I'll be here for you, no matter what. I learned that from my brother. Ryan was always there for me. He did a good job, and he was only a year older than me. I've got thirty-seven years on you, kid."

He looked at her again. "Thirty-seven. Does that sound old to you?" Not surprisingly, she didn't answer.

He drew in a breath. He couldn't remember ever being this unsure of himself. He didn't want to break her or hurt her in some way. How did people become parents more than once? The task seemed so daunting. Maybe it got easier with practice. He could only hope.

He turned right at the next signal and entered his neighborhood. Ryan had wanted to come along while he picked up his daughter, but Ronni had said he had to do this by himself. The sooner he got used to being alone with her, the better for the both of them.

Tanner frowned. "We can't keep calling you 'her' or 'the baby.' We're going to have to come up with a name. I wish you could tell me what you'd like…or at least what you'd hate."

He pulled into his driveway, which circled in front of the large, two-story house.

"This is it," he said as he switched off the engine. "You're home."

His daughter wasn't overly impressed. She continued to sleep as he unstrapped her car seat. He slung the bag of supplies the hospital had sent home with him over one shoulder, then picked up the seat and carried it, and his daughter, inside.

Ryan and Ronni were waiting in the foyer. "How did it go?" his brother asked.

"Okay." He let the bag slip to the floor and held out the carrier. "Here she is." He stared down doubtfully. "She's sleeping."

"Don't complain. She'll be up soon enough. Come see what we did."

He followed them upstairs and into his daughter's room. While he'd been gone Ryan had finished putting together the three-drawer changing table and Ronni had put all the clothes and linens away.

"Newborn size clothes are in the top drawer," she said, pulling it open to show him. "Everything else is in the lower drawers. Oh, and I hung the dress in the closet."

He glanced over his shoulder and saw the tiny dress hanging alone on the rack. It looked impossibly small and foreign. He sucked in his breath.

"I, ah, guess I'd better get her in bed," he said.

"Absolutely. I washed the sheets and the comforter. They've only been out of the dryer a few minutes, so they're probably even still warm," she said helpfully.

Tanner glanced at Ryan, but his brother shook his head. "You're going to have to learn how to do this sometime. Might as well be now."

Tanner grunted because the alternative was to say something unpleasant and he'd already promised his daughter he wasn't going to do that.

First he unfastened the straps holding her in place. Carefully, supporting his baby's head the way Ronni and the nurse at the hospital had shown him, he lifted her from the car seat and cradled her against the crook of his arm. Then he crossed the room and gently put her in the crib.

She barely stirred. Then her big blue eyes opened, she wiggled once, yawned, then drifted off to sleep.

"I guess you're really a dad now," Ryan said and slapped him on the back. "Congratulations."

"Thanks. I've got to do something about a name." He glanced at his brother. "I was thinking about Cecilia after our mother. I like it, but it sounds stuffy for such a little girl, so I was thinking that would be her real name but we'd call her Lia."

Ryan nodded. "I like it."

"Me, too," said Ronni, then sniffed. "Let's go downstairs. If I stay here much longer, I'm going to cry. You know, hormones, babies, it's inevitable."

Both men hustled her out of the room. They went downstairs into the family room, then Tanner remembered the baby monitor and had to run back up to get it. He turned on the unit on the dresser, clicked on the one in his hand, and paused by the crib.

"Hi, Lia," he murmured. "I'm glad you're sleeping. You should think about sleeping a lot. That would give your old man a break. Want to give it a try?"

Then because he couldn't help himself, he stroked the back of his index finger against her cheek. The warm skin was so incredibly soft. She barely stirred.

"I don't usually fall this fast, kid, but you seem to have a firm grip on my heart. I guess we're stuck with each other."

Despite the fear, he knew then that there was no where else he would rather be.

Chapter Five

Tanner glanced at his watch as he walked down the stairs. It had been all of twenty minutes, and so far, so good. If the next twenty years would go as smoothly, he might just get the hang of this whole parenting thing.

As he stepped into the family room, he saw Ronni leaning against Ryan. His brother had his arms around his fiancée, and they were talking quietly. Nothing about their posture was sexual, yet Tanner sensed the intimacy between them. Something in his gut told him that Ryan had been lucky enough, or smart enough, to find another extraordinary woman to share his life. Ryan's first wife, Patricia, had been a model wife and mother. Personality wise, Ronni was a lot different, but in her heart she was just as loving.

Tanner pushed down the surge of envy that appeared unexpectedly. He reminded himself that he'd never been one for commitments. Of course he'd never gotten the point of kids either and now he had one. Everything changed.

Ryan glanced up and saw him. "Ronni and I are going to let you off the hook about baby-sitting the kids," he said.

Tanner stared blankly. "What are you talking about?"

Ryan grinned. "See, that's what happens. You get a child in the house and the parents start losing their minds. The first thing to go is short-term memory. Trust me on this. It's only going to get worse."

Ronni shook her head. "What your big brother is trying to say is that the wedding is at the end of the month. With a newborn in the house, you're not really in a position to take care of three more children."

Tanner set the baby monitor on the counter closest to the family room and ran his fingers through his hair. "You're right. I did forget." When Ryan and Ronni had decided to elope, he'd offered to take Ryan's children for the long weekend. Lily, Ryan's mother-in-law and his usual source for live-in help, was going to be taking a cruise with her sister.

"Look, this is your wedding," Tanner said. "I still want to take the kids. Drew's a big help with his younger brother and sister and I don't want you two worrying. You're barely going to get away for more than a weekend as it is."

Ryan and Ronni exchanged a look. "We'll find someone else," Ronni said firmly. "It's sweet of you to offer, but you have no idea what you're getting into. Having a baby in the house changes everything. We'll arrange child-care for Ryan's three.'' She glanced at her watch, then at Ryan. ''We need to be going,'' she said.

Ryan nodded. ''She's right.'' He tapped his shirt pocket. ''I've got my cell phone with me, so call if you need anything.''

They were leaving? Tanner fought down a sudden surge of panic. ''You guys can stay a little longer, can't you?''

''Sorry.'' Ronni picked up her purse and slung it over one shoulder. ''I'll be in touch later this afternoon with a couple of numbers for baby nurses. I have two in mind and I think one of them is available.''

He watched helplessly as they headed for the front door. ''What do I do if she wakes up?''

''Take care of her,'' Ronni said. ''Check her diaper, then feed her.''

''I don't know how.''

''Yes, you do. We went over it this morning.''

Yeah, right, like practicing on a doll was the same as feeding a baby. ''But...''

''Be sure to check the temperature of the formula and burp her when you're done,'' Ronni said, giving him a reassuring smile. ''If you get into trouble, call on the cell phone. Ryan and I can be back here in less than twenty minutes.''

He would prefer they didn't leave at all, but he couldn't bring himself to insist that they stay.

''Sure,'' he said with a confidence he didn't feel. ''We'll be fine.''

They waved, then walked out the front door. Tanner wanted to go running after them and beg them to move in with him for the next two or three years.

Maybe he should ask Ronni to find a baby nurse who could start today, or in the next fifteen minutes.

He paced the length of the family room, then turned and stared at the baby monitor. It was just a matter of time until Lia woke up and started crying. Dear God, then what was he going to do?

Kelly took the stairs down to the basement. Once there, she headed for the cafeteria. The delivery had gone smoothly, and mother and child were doing well. As soon as she had something to eat she would head over to Tanner's. After all, as the grumbling in her stomach reminded her, her page had come before she'd had a chance to eat any of the bagels she'd bought that morning.

The cafeteria was mostly empty. Kelly collected a tray then filled it with a bowl of fruit, a small salad and a roast beef sandwich. After paying, she looked around and saw a familiar doctor sitting at a table by the wall. She smiled at the sight of her friend, Dr. Alexandra Larson, and walked over.

"Hi. Are you on call?" Kelly asked as she set her tray on the table.

Alex glanced up. Her normally bright brown eyes were shadowed from lack of sleep and there wasn't a scrap of makeup on her face. She smiled wearily. "This is my weekend and I was called in just after midnight. A car accident. A van hit a small pick-up. Everyone survived, but I had a couple of difficult breaks to fix." Alex was an orthopedic surgeon. She picked up a cup of coffee and took a sip. "What's your excuse for being here on Saturday?"

Kelly took a seat. "The usual," she said. "A six-pound eight-ounce baby boy. He's about as cute as

can be and the parents are so happy they're floating."

Alex rested her elbow on the table and leaned her
chin on her hand. Her hair, a short wedge of auburn
tinted brown, swayed with the movement. "Must be
nice to get instant gratification from your patients.
Mine stay asleep while I work to repair whatever
the problem is. Afterwards, they're often groggy and
in pain. No one ever floats. I'd like floating. Or even
applause."

Kelly laughed. "I confess, I've never had applause. It would be nice. Maybe a gallery of impressed bystanders."

"Fans," Alex said firmly. "Just like rock stars."
She stared at Kelly. "You look happy about something and it's not just work."

Kelly was surprised. "I do? What do you mean?"

"I'm not sure. There's this glow." Her brown
eyes narrowed. "Either there's a new man in your
life, or you just had a make-over. If it's the latter, I
want to know where you went. Maybe they can do
something for me. I need a change from my wash-
and-wear life."

"You adore your life and you don't want to
change a thing." Kelly took a bite of her sandwich
and chewed. There wasn't a man in her life, she
thought, even as a blush crept its way up her cheeks.
Tanner wasn't really in her life. She was just helping
him out with a difficult situation. The fact that he
was good-looking and had an amazing butt was interesting, but not important. She swallowed.

"Things are going well for me," Kelly said. "I
love my work, I've settled into living here in Honeygrove. I guess that's what you're seeing. Con-

tentment. Now speaking of men, how's your favorite guy?''

Alex's expression softened and her full lips curved up in a tender smile. ''Tyler is perfect in every way.'' She laughed. ''Okay, he can make me crazy in about thirty seconds, but other than that, he's wonderful. I thought three was a great age, but four is even better. He's so smart.'' She paused, then laughed again. ''I'm gushing.''

''You always gush about Tyler. It's charming. It proves you're a great mother.''

Alex sighed and leaned back in her chair. ''I try. Time is always a problem. I'm so busy with work. But he's my world.''

Kelly thought about that statement. Tyler *was* his mother's world. Alex had never married and Kelly didn't know much about Tyler's father. She wanted to ask if Alex ever thought about having a man in her life—a grown-up, in addition to her charming son. Did she ever get lonely? Most of the time Kelly didn't allow herself to think of those kind of questions, but lately they'd been popping up more and more frequently. She'd come to realize that sometimes she needed more than just her work.

Except if she asked Alex those questions, Alex would also ask them of her and she wasn't ready to answer them. So instead she asked about Alex's houseguest.

''Are things still going well with Wendy?''

''Sure. She's a sweetheart. And huge,'' Alex added. ''I swear that baby's going to pop out any second.''

''I'm guessing in the next week or so.''

"She's staying with me until the baby is about six weeks old," Alex said.

"Thanks for taking her in." Kelly smiled at her friend. "You were a real lifesaver."

Alex shrugged. "That's what spare rooms are for."

Not for most people, Kelly thought. Alex was someone special. Her friend's guest room had a revolving door. As soon as one person in need left, another one showed up. Alex didn't turn anyone away. When Kelly had realized Wendy, all of seventeen years old and eight months pregnant, had been thrown out and was living on the streets, she'd instantly called Alex. And Alex had taken her in.

"I owe you," Kelly said. "And I mean that. I would have taken her home myself, but not only do I not have a spare room, my apartment is too close to Wendy's mom's place. She wouldn't have been safe there."

"Oh, stop," Alex told her. "I can read that look in your eyes. Don't you dare start talking about what a bleeding heart I am. This is where I remind you that you're the one who volunteers at that clinic, giving away your very valuable time for free. The way I see it, we're both doing what's right. End of story."

"Okay. I won't grovel in thanks, but I do appreciate what you've done."

Alex dismissed her with a wave, then pressed her fingers to her mouth to smother a yawn. "I'm going to head home and see if I can get a couple of hours of sleep before Tyler comes home from the sitter. What are you doing with the rest of your weekend?"

"Helping a friend," Kelly said casually, ignoring

the flare of excitement Alex's question had stirred. Tanner was just a friend, and there was nothing between them. Nothing except her imagination and too much time between men.

"Hush, Lia," Tanner pleaded as he rocked his daughter in his arms.

When she'd awakened a little more than an hour before, he'd rushed upstairs at the first whisper of her cry. He'd checked her diaper, which had been dry, then had carefully fed her. After double-checking the temperature of the formula, he'd positioned her as both Ronni and the nurse in the hospital had shown him. Lia had taken to the bottle with no trouble at all. When she'd finished her meal, he'd held her against his shoulder and patted her back until she'd let out an impressive burp. But since then, all she'd done was cry.

The harsh, hiccuping sound made him frantic. Did she have a temperature? Was she sick? Had he given her too much formula or not enough?

She drew in her breath and let out another sob. Her face was all scrunched up, with her eyes squeezed tightly closed and her tiny fists waving in the air.

"No one should be this unhappy," he murmured to her as he rocked her back and forth. In the past twenty minutes it felt as if her weight had doubled. He paced the length of the downstairs and wondered if he should just give up and page Ronni.

Before he could decide, the doorbell rang. He rushed to the foyer and pulled it open.

Kelly stood on the porch holding several plastic grocery bags. "I brought supplies," she said over the sound of Lia's crying. "From the drugstore. Baby wash, diaper wipes, that sort of thing." She stepped into the entrance and glanced at Lia. "What's wrong?"

He resisted the urge to hold out the screaming child to her to fix. "I don't know. When she woke up, she was fine. I fed her then burped her. I thought she'd go back to sleep."

Kelly crossed to the kitchen where she set down her bags. "What about her diaper?"

"I checked it first thing."

Kelly began unpacking the bags. He clamped down on his frustration. How could she be so calm about this? Something could be seriously wrong with Lia. Didn't she want to recommend that he rush her to the emergency room?

"Did you check her diaper after you fed her?"

He blinked at the question. "After?"

She gave him a quick smile. "Sometimes babies go after they eat, rather than before. Sometimes they go both times. Have you checked recently?"

Just then he caught the odor of some-thing…something not pleasant. He swallowed. "Do I have to?"

"Oh yes. And before you think of passing that job off on me, I'll just go ahead and mention I have a lot more stuff in my car. I'll bring it in right now."

With that, she disappeared.

Tanner stared at his daughter. "About this poop thing," he said. "I'm not up to it. Maybe you should just dispose of everything in liquid form. What do you think?"

She gave another cry, so he headed up the stairs. Two minutes later he had her on the changing table and was staring at something that looked like a prop out of an alien horror movie.

"What is it?" he asked when he heard Kelly's footsteps in the hall. "It's disgusting."

"It's something you're going to have to get used to." She poked her head into the bedroom and grinned. "It could be worse."

He looked up. "How?"

"She could be a boy. They are notorious for sending up a little shower while they're having their diaper changed."

"Great," he muttered returning his attention to his daughter. "There are too many firsts for me, sweet Lia. Bringing you home, your first bottle, now this first diaper. Things are moving too fast. Let's all just relax for a bit and catch up, okay?"

She'd stopped crying. He gently wiped her bottom, then collected a tiny new diaper and set it into place. Her gaze seemed to look at his face and as usual, her expression was faintly worried.

"I think she knows I'm clueless," he told Kelly. "She's got this look on her face as if she's sure I'm going to drop her or something."

"All babies do that," Kelly said, walking over and smiling down at Lia. "I heard your daddy call you by a name. Lia. Do you like it?"

Lia responded by fluttering her eyelids a couple of times, then dozing off.

"I'll take that as a yes," Kelly said.

He glanced at her and saw she carried an armful of supplies. He saw baby wash, baby shampoo, cotton balls and swabs, tiny washcloths and a host of other boxes and jars he didn't want to even think about. Babies required way too much stuff as it was.

How was he supposed to keep it all straight? What if he used the wrong product on the wrong part?

"Don't go there," she warned as he buttoned Lia back into her sleeper.

"Go where?"

"You're getting nervous. I can see it in your eyes."

Her own eyes were a hazel brown, but this close he could see tiny flecks of gold in the irises. They were wide and pretty, and perfectly set off by the fringe of bangs falling almost to her eyebrows. She didn't wear any makeup that he could see. Even so, her lashes were long and thick, and her skin smooth.

He picked up Lia and held her in his arms. "I don't want to get it wrong."

Kelly nodded at the sleeping infant. "So far, so good. Why don't you set her down and I'll go put this stuff in her bathroom."

He watched as Kelly crossed the room and disappeared through the doorway, then he carefully set his daughter into her crib. She barely stirred as he pulled the comforter up to her chest, then checked the baby monitor. Kelly met him in the hall.

"I've put the bath supplies on the counter. For the next few months you'll be using a small baby tub and I wasn't sure if you'd do that in her room or downstairs in the kitchen sink."

"The kitchen sink? She's not a piece of zucchini."

Kelly grinned. "I know, but the sink is at least at a decent height. With the bathtub, you'll be all bent over."

"Oh. I hadn't thought of that." But then there were dozens of things he hadn't thought of yet. Like the baby monitor. He checked it to make sure it was turned on, then led Kelly down to the family room.

There were more shopping bags waiting there. He stared at the pile. "Please tell me that everything comes with instructions," he said.

"Pretty much. And if it doesn't, you'll find out about it in the baby book I gave you. Or you can ask me while I'm here."

"Ronni's getting me a baby nurse," he said, hoping the nurse would arrive soon with about fifteen years of experience. "So I can ask her, as well."

"You're all covered."

He still felt like he was a non-swimmer who'd been thrown into the ocean, but he didn't tell her that. "Want something to drink?" he asked, walking into the kitchen and pulling open the refrigerator door. "I have different sodas."

"Anything diet?" she asked.

He glanced at her, at her long legs in tailored slacks and the casual shirt she'd tucked into the waistband. She was tall, athletic looking and very appealing.

"Sure," he said. "But tell me why?"

She glanced down at herself and laughed. "I'm not on a diet, if that's what you mean, but one of the reasons is I'm cautious about what I eat. I choose my calories carefully and to me, soda is a waste. So I prefer the low-cal version."

He made a face, but pulled out a can for her. When he reached for a glass, she snagged the container from him. "I never bother," she said. "It just means something more to put in the dishwasher and something more to return to the cupboard."

"A woman after my own heart," he said, collecting a regular cola drink for himself and following her back into the family room.

Kelly settled on one end of the sofa, while he took the other. Afternoon sunlight spilled into the room making her medium blond hair seem a little lighter. He'd only ever seen her with her hair pulled back into a braid, or fastened up on her head. He wondered how long it was when it was loose and how it would look tumbling around her face.

The image produced instant heat inside of him. He realized then how distracted he'd been with Lia. He'd been alone with Kelly several times in the past couple of days and hadn't been able to appreciate that she was funny, intelligent and easy on the eye. Not that he was interested in her that way. She was helping out and he was grateful. They were friends, nothing more. They had to be. For one thing, Kelly wasn't his type. For another, he had a child to think of now. He couldn't keep practicing his own version of serial monogamy. Lia would get confused.

He popped the top on his soda. "I almost forgot to ask," he said. "How was the delivery?"

Kelly sighed as her face took on a look of radiance. "It was great. Everything went perfectly." She paused. "The mother might take issue with that. After all, she spent several hours in labor. But the birth was smooth and easy on the baby. They had a healthy little boy and both the parents are thrilled." She looked at him. "Usually when I deliver a child, I rarely get to see him or her again, so it's nice to be able to follow-up with one of my babies. Lia is doing very well."

"I hope so. She seems okay. I'm glad that Ronni's going to be her pediatrician."

"Nothing like having a doctor in the family?" Kelly asked.

"Exactly."

She leaned back against the sofa. "So how did you pick Lia for her name?"

"Actually, her real name is Cecilia after my mom, but I thought we could call her Lia. It's a little more contemporary, not to mention easier for her to spell."

"That's so nice. Your mom must be thrilled."

Tanner set his soda on the coffee table. "My parents are both dead. They died when Ryan and I were really young. I thought you knew, although I'm not sure why you would."

Kelly frowned. "You're right. I did know, I think. I must have forgotten…" Her voice trailed off, then her expression cleared. "I remember where I heard that. It was a couple of months ago. At the Heart Ball. When your brother gave his speech about the new wing."

Tanner nodded. He remembered that evening. Just a short time before both he and his brother had received word that the funding for the construction of the hospital wing had fallen through when one of the officers of the foundation had run off with millions. Tanner had been paying his contractors out of his own pocket, with the understanding that the next installment of funds would arrive on time. When it hadn't, work on the hospital wing had halted.

For several weeks, he'd balanced on the verge of bankruptcy. Ryan had moved mountains to arrange for alternative funding. Of the forty million they'd needed to complete the work, Ryan had found all but five million. Work had started back and now they were scrambling to finish the project on time. Tanner knew his brother would come through with the rest of the money.

"How's everything going with that?" Kelly asked. "I heard that it was pretty bad for a while."

"We should still make the September first deadline. It's the twentieth anniversary of the hospital, so I'm doing my best to make sure the dedication ceremony can go on as planned."

"Didn't you almost lose your company because of the loss of funding?"

"It was dicey for a while," he admitted. "But I trusted my brother. Ryan said he would find the money—and that's his job. So I hung on until the funds came through. Now it's just a matter of finishing up the work."

The phone rang. He reached for it and spoke into the receiver. "Hello?"

He listened as a man on the other end talked for a couple of minutes. Tanner started laughing. "Yeah. I wish I could tell you otherwise, but they're mine." He paused and listened. "No, I appreciate you following up on them. Thanks." He hung up. "You're not going to believe who that was," he said.

"Tell me."

"My credit card company. They wanted to confirm a very large charge to a baby store. Apparently that purchase didn't match my normal charging pattern and the computer flagged my account."

She laughed. "They'd better get used to that kind of thing with you. There's going to be lots more for you to buy."

"I don't want to think about it."

She picked up the teddy bear that Ronni and Ryan had brought for Lia. "Isn't he a charmer," she said, smoothing the soft fur around the stuffed animal's face. "Bears have always been my favorite."

Her expression turned wistful as she rubbed the animal's head.

"Tell me again why you don't have a dozen kids of your own," he said impulsively.

Something dark and painful slipped across her eyes. Then she blinked and it was gone. "Interesting question for which I don't have an equally interesting answer," she said lightly. "But you're the important one right now. I want to know how you're feeling. Is the panic under control?"

"Seems to be," he said, recognizing that she was deliberately changing the subject but not sure he should let her. Then he remembered that she was being kind enough to give up one of her weekends to help him with his daughter. He owed her. More importantly, her personal life was none of his business.

He glanced at his watch. "Hour four of having her home and all is well."

"I'm glad." She stood up. "I thought I could go to the grocery store. I'm guessing you don't have a lot of food in the house and it's not as if you can go out easily. Then I'm available to assist with the baby care. That is if you still want me to stay over."

"Are you kidding? I won't make it without you."

She smiled. "Then what about making a list?"

But even as he went through his cupboards and figured out what he had and what he needed, he couldn't get those words out of his head. *I won't make it without you.* They'd both known what he meant when he said it. He was talking about Lia and his lack of parental experience. Nothing more. But for a moment he wondered how his life would be different if he could for once allow himself to really need someone.

Chapter Six

Kelly stirred and rolled over. She opened her eyes and saw that it was a little after two in the morning. She blinked as she looked at the unfamiliar room. This wasn't her apartment and it wasn't the hospital. Where...

Then her memory returned. She was at Tanner's house, in one of the spare bedrooms. Unlike Lia's room, this one hadn't been remodeled. Old-fashioned wallpaper still covered the walls, contrasting with the heavy drapes on the window.

Kelly stretched and tried to figure out what had awakened her. Was it Lia? She looked at the clock again. She'd expected to be up before now to help Tanner, or even take over one of the feedings. Oh well, now that she was awake, she might as well check on the baby.

Kelly threw back the covers and stood up. She'd

deliberately worn sweats and a T-shirt to bed so all she had to do was fumble for her slippers and slide them on. She tucked a loose strand of hair behind her ear and made her way into the hall.

The house was all shadows. Lia's door stood open and she could see the faint light from a Disney nightlite illuminating a patch of hardwood flooring. As she stepped into the room, a slight movement caught her attention. She looked up and saw Tanner standing by the window.

Kelly froze in place, staring. Tanner wore jeans and nothing else. He held his tiny daughter in his arms, cradling her against his bare chest and rocking her gently. Moonlight filtered through the half-open blinds, highlighting, then shading, the shape of his shoulders, the muscles in his arms, the warm color of his skin.

Deep in her stomach, something stirred to life. Some small producer of female hormones, some long dormant cells secreted a long since forgotten bit of magic that made a woman want a man. She felt the first flickering of desire, but it was more than that. Her attraction wasn't just to the perfectly muscled body but also to the tenderness inherent in those incredibly strong hands. A woman could trust a man who held a baby with such tenderness.

She knew she hadn't made a sound, but Tanner turned toward her. "Did I wake you?" he asked softly. "I tried to be quiet."

"It wasn't noise that got my attention," she admitted, "but the absence of it. I came to check on Lia."

"Great minds," he said. "That's what I was doing. She was awake and looked hungry, so I got her a bottle, then changed her diaper. She ate great and is already back to sleep.'' He smiled. ''I couldn't figure out why she was sleeping so much, but then I got a look at her diaper. It must take a lot of energy to produce all that waste product.''

Kelly laughed. ''Waste product, huh? Interesting way to describe it.''

In the semi-darkness she couldn't see the color of his eyes, but she knew it. Malone blue. He was the kind of man women dreamed about meeting—handsome, charming, successful. So why was he awake at two in the morning holding a child?

''Who are you Tanner Malone?'' she asked before she could stop herself.

''You mean why me, why her?'' he asked, nodding at Lia. ''I guess I'm just one man who wants to do the right thing. I'm terrified, but trying.''

''That's all anyone can ask of you.''

''Oh, I think Lia is going to have more expectations than that, but I have some time before I have to worry about them.''

She'd been wrong about him. She realized that now. All those months she'd been Lucy's doctor, listening to her patient grumble about the guy who'd knocked her up and had then insisted she have the baby, but who didn't want responsibility for it. Kelly had been furious with both of them for being careless during sex, but she'd been more angry with Tanner. It was easy for men, because they didn't get pregnant. They just walked away from the problem. Except Tanner hadn't.

She leaned against the door frame and crossed her arms over her chest. ''I was wrong about you,'' she said, her voice low. ''I've been angry at you for most of Lucy's pregnancy. I thought you were an irresponsible bastard who'd gotten caught and wanted out. But I was wrong about all of it. I'm sorry, Tanner.''

He was quiet for a long time, just staring at her in the darkness and rocking Lia. ''Thank you for apologizing,'' he said at last. ''That means a lot to me. But you were also right about me. Not about me being irresponsible. We used a condom, and as an obstetrician, I'm sure you're very aware that they sometimes fail. But about the rest of it. When Lucy told me she was pregnant, I didn't know what to think.''

He turned back to the window. Kelly didn't feel that he was shutting her out as much as protecting himself. As if he was embarrassed or ashamed of what he was saying. She wanted to go to him and touch him, tell him that she understood. But they didn't know each other that well. Instead, she stood her ground and waited.

''The entire relationship was a mistake. In fact calling it a relationship gives it more credit than it deserves. It was the Fourth of July weekend. We met at a party. I hadn't had a woman in my life for a long time. It was hot, we were both in the mood, and then suddenly we were doing it. I knew it was dumb even then, but what the hell, right?'' He glanced down at his daughter. ''Sorry, sweetie, I know I'm not supposed to swear.''

''You don't have to tell me this,'' Kelly said, more because she thought she should than because she didn't want to know.

''Probably not, but I think it's important infor-mation.'' He walked over to the crib and set Lia down on her back. "We said good-bye and I never expected to see her again. About two months later she called to tell me she was pregnant. Apparently she'd been debating whether or not to inform me for a couple of weeks. I think her plan had been to go get an abortion and get on with her life."

Kelly thought about Lucy and realized Tanner had summed up the other woman fairly accurately. Lucy had not been thrilled to be pregnant.

"I didn't want her to do that," he said. "I didn't want the kid, either, but I wanted her to carry it to term." He leaned over and stroked his daughter's cheek. "Thank God. Lucy fought me, but eventually I convinced her. I promised to cover all the out-of-pocket medical expenses her policy didn't. We both agreed to give the baby up for adoption."

He glanced at Kelly. In the dimly lit room, it was impossible to see what he was thinking. "I swear that's what I planned to do. Right up until the day she was born. Then something happened. I guess she went from being an abstraction to something real. And I couldn't walk away from that...or her."

Kelly dropped her arms to her sides. "I feel responsible for a part of that," she said. "If I hadn't let you hold her, you wouldn't have bonded."

His teeth flashed white. "I don't think so. While it would be really nice to be able to blame you, it's not your fault. If I hadn't wanted Lia, all the holding in the world wouldn't have changed my mind."

Kelly wasn't so sure. "Something happens when a parent holds his or her newborn for the first time."

"Do you think holding her would have changed Lucy's mind?"

His quiet question made her pause. She'd checked

her patient before Lucy had been released. The younger woman had expressed only relief at having her pregnancy behind her. She hadn't mentioned anything about the baby or what was happening to her.

"No, I don't," she admitted.

"So that proves my point." He straightened. "Tell you what, Doc, you can be guilty about any number of things in your life, but you're going to have to let this one go. You're not responsible for Lia." He motioned to the room. "But I do owe you. You've been a great help and I want to return the favor. I can fix the plumbing, remodel a bathroom, hang wallpaper, you name it."

"I'll have to let you know," Kelly said, thinking of her small, spare apartment. The management company handled any maintenance problems she had. As for remodeling or wallpaper, she'd never done much of anything to make her three-room place a home. For her it was utilitarian, nothing more.

"You do that," he said. "Because I'm not going to forget what I owe you."

Somewhere in the house a clock chimed.

"It's late," Tanner told her. "We'd better get to bed and get some sleep while we can. I have a feeling this little girl is going to be up a couple more times before sunrise."

"You're right."

She turned to leave. At least that was her intent, but somehow her gaze got locked with his. She told herself to look away, to start walking back to her room, but she couldn't move. Her legs were too heavy and those suddenly awake hormones were busy swaying through her body, leaving her weak and wanting.

As she watched, his attention seemed to drift downward...toward her mouth. She told herself it was her imagination. That he wasn't thinking about kissing her anymore than she was thinking about being in his arms. That she didn't wonder about how strong he would feel, or the warmth of his bare skin under her fingers. And that she'd never even once fantasized about the firmness of his lips or how his tongue would taste.

Then, because her thoughts both frightened and excited her, she turned on her heel and escaped.

"So when can I buy one of the backpack baby carriers?" Tanner asked. He sat on one of the stools and leaned his forearms on the counter that divided the kitchen from the family room.

Kelly stood at the stove stirring spaghetti sauce. She inhaled the spicy-sweet fragrance. In another hour or so, it would be finished. They would have some tonight and she would freeze the rest for Tanner to heat up. If he'd thought he'd eaten on the run before, he was in for a shock. There was nothing like having a baby around to interfere with regularly scheduled meals.

"She has to be able to hold up her head," Kelly told him. "You can get the front kind of baby pack fairly soon. They protect the infant's neck more."

"Right." He made a note on the pad of paper in front of him.

"How's the list coming?" she asked.

"Not bad. I can't believe I have to go to that baby

store again. I didn't think there was anything we *hadn't* bought.''

Kelly laughed. ''Babies are like that. But you're getting the hang of it.''

He looked at the baby monitor, then at his watch. ''I'm starting to. I figure we've got another half hour before we hear the first stirrings from Lia. At least she's sleeping a bunch. I like that. Now if only she'd stop leaving that junk in her diaper.''

''You'll get used to it.''

''Maybe. The thing is, I don't want to.''

Tanner's grin was boyish and contagious. Kelly had to turn her attention back to her sauce before she said or did something stupid. She'd been in Tanner's house barely twenty-four hours and already the man was getting to her. Knowing why didn't make him easier to resist.

It was just situational, she thought. Being around a man bonding with a baby was fairly irresistible. Then there was the additional problem of her life. She'd spent most of it living like a nun. She didn't encourage men and she wasn't beautiful enough that they came on to her regardless of the signals she sent. Add to that her impossible schedule throughout her years in medical school and during her residency. All together, it made perfect sense for her to respond to the first good-looking single guy to do more than say hi to her.

The trick would be keeping him from figuring it out. While she liked being friends with Tanner, she did not want him feeling sorry for her. She didn't know what his type was, but she was reasonably confident it wasn't her. He would prefer flashier women. Those who had time to develop a sense of style and adventure. She was cotton sensible and not the least bit romantic. He would want Miss July with a brain.

"We need to get some toys," Tanner said, continuing to work on his list. "Lia has the mobile above her bed and the bear that Ronni and Ryan brought. I definitely want another mobile for above the changing table, but that's not enough." He tapped his pen against the counter. "She's too young for dolls, right?"

"Just a little." Kelly shook her head. "She's a newborn. Toys are not a big priority right now."

"But they will be. What about all that educational stuff? So she can learn to recognize shapes and colors. When does that start?"

"Not this week. In fact the most exciting event you can look forward to in the next month is her lifting up her head while she's on her stomach."

"Okay. So she won't be reading anytime soon, but I still want to buy her some toys."

She glanced at him over her shoulder. "You know that Lia shouldn't go out into crowded places for a few more days. You don't want her exposed to a lot of germs."

Tanner looked insulted. "I'm hardly going to take her to the toy store with me. Then they won't be a surprise."

Kelly didn't know whether to laugh at him or throw the spoon she was holding. "A surprise? You think she'll notice?"

"Of course. She's an incredibly bright baby. I would have thought as a doctor you would have recognized that already." He jotted down a couple more items. "I'll either go at lunch, or ask Mrs.

Dawson to stay an extra half hour while I stop at the toy store on my way home.''

Mrs. Dawson was the baby nurse Ronni had recommended. The lovely older woman had stopped by that morning to meet both Tanner and Lia. She was gentle, experienced and had enough credentials and recommendations to get a job with a visiting head of state.

''Are you sure you don't want Mrs. Dawson to stay at night?'' she asked. Tanner had surprised her by requesting the baby nurse take care of Lia only during the day.

''No, but I want to try it that way first. If I can't get any sleep, I'll have to have her stay longer. But I want to get used to taking care of my daughter myself. As soon as she's old enough, I'll bring her to the office with me. I've got several recommendations for day care for times when bringing her to work is impossible.'' He shrugged. ''It's not a perfect solution, but I'm willing to be flexible until I find what works best for both of us.''

''Very impressive,'' Kelly told him. ''Less than a week ago you had no plans to keep her and now you're pulling it all together.''

''I don't have a choice.''

''That's true. Once you decided to keep her, you were stuck. But you're still handling it well.'' She knew that if she'd met him at a party, she would have dismissed him as too good-looking to be anything but self-centered and shallow. But Kelly would have been the shallow one by making that judgment without getting to know him. She also would have been wrong.

She turned down the heat on her spaghetti sauce,

picked up her glass of wine and walked over to the counter where Tanner worked. It was surprisingly easy to spend time with him. She'd been worried that the weekend might be awkward, but she'd enjoyed herself very much.

"All right, Mr. Malone, it's time for you to spill the beans. Why don't you have a wife and half a dozen kids, or at least three, like your brother?"

He set down his pen and looked at her. "Not my style."

She motioned to the kitchen. "Confirmed bachelors don't remodel. At least they don't remodel a perfect home for a family. You told me you don't cook very much, but look at this kitchen. You did a terrific job."

"For resale."

"Liar," she said softly. His blue eyes were the most amazing shade, she thought, wishing she could get lost inside them. "I've heard about your reputation with women. You can't be lacking in offers for permanent roommates."

He shrugged, then took a drink of his wine. "It never worked out that way. I've always had long term relationships that just ended."

"Did you know they would end when you started?"

"What?"

She leaned against the counter. "I have this theory about people who practice serial monogamy. Most of the time they aren't interested in a permanent commitment, but they don't want to admit that. So they find someone who appears to have all the qualities they could want in a mate. They go out for a few months or even a few years, then something happens. There's a fatal flaw and they break up. Later, when they talk about the relationship, they always mention knowing from the beginning that something was wrong. Instead of looking for Mr. or Ms. Right, they are secretly searching for the almost-right person who has a fatal flaw. That way they look like they're trying to get involved, but they're really not.''

He frowned. ''That's pretty twisted.''

''Does it sound right?''

''I'm not sure. Ryan did the wife and family thing, but it was never anything I wanted.''

''Has that changed? You have a daughter now.''

''Tell me about it.'' He took another sip of wine. ''Things have to be different. I know I'm going to have to be more careful about who I let into our lives now that it's not just me. If I want a relationship, I'll need to find someone who will be accepting of Lia, too.''

''That won't be a problem,'' Kelly said.

He leaned toward her. ''I have to ask you a question. As a woman, I mean.''

''All right.''

He took a deep breath. ''What am I supposed to tell Lia about her mother? I'm not upset about Lucy's decision. In fact, I'm glad she's gone. She never wanted to have children and I don't think she would have been very patient with a baby. But I don't want to say that to Lia. I don't want to tell her that her mother didn't want her. I never want her to know that Lucy thought about having an abortion and that I had to talk her out of it. How is a kid supposed to survive knowing that?''

Kelly felt as if all the blood had rushed out of

her. She felt cold and light-headed. She'd had this exact conversation with herself a thousand times in the past. Maybe more.

"Some mothers don't give up their children so easily," she said, working hard to keep her voice steady. "Some spend the rest of their lives wondering if they did the right thing."

"Maybe." Tanner sounded doubtful. "That still doesn't answer my question. How do I tell Lia that her mother didn't want her?"

Kelly took a step back. "I can't help you with this," she said. "Maybe you should talk to Ryan or Ronni. Maybe a child psychologist could help. It's not something you have to deal with for a while."

"I guess not." He stared at her. "Are you all right?"

She wanted to leave, to run away and hide. Except she'd done that before and the problem always followed her. So instead she straightened her spine and squared her shoulders.

"I'm fine. Your question caught me off guard because it's something I've thought a lot about."

"Because you deliver babies who are going to be given up for adoption," he said. "I understand."

"No, you don't. I've thought about this because I once gave up a child."

Chapter Seven

Kelly figured she'd already started down the road of telling the truth, so she might as well continue. "It was a long time ago," she said. "I was all of seventeen when I got pregnant. It was difficult for me then and to be honest, it's still a little tough to talk about."

She risked a glance at Tanner, then wished she hadn't. He was staring at her wide-eyed, his face a mask of stunned surprise. She folded her arms over her chest. This is why she didn't share the details of her past with many people. So few of them understood.

He continued to stare at her. She had to dig down deep to find enough anger to combat her hurt. So he was going to judge her. She shouldn't have expected anything else…except she had. She'd thought Tanner might understand.

"You weren't there," she said crisply. "You can't know what it's like."

"I never said I could," he told her. "I don't think less of you, I'm just..."

"Surprised, shocked, disapproving?"

"None of those." He placed his hands flat on the counter and stared at her. "Never anything like that. I have great respect for you, Kelly. If I'm feeling anything it's that I'm relieved to find out you're human, just like the rest of us. Until five minutes ago, I'd assumed you were one of those annoying, perfect people. You know the kind—always showing everyone up with their neatly planned lives. You're everything I could never be. I can't believe you made a mistake."

"I'm just a regular person." She bit her lower lip, not sure she could believe him. Was he really not judging her?

"You're not like the rest of us," he said. "Look at you. You're a gifted doctor. You've saved dozens of lives, maybe more. You committed yourself to years of schooling when most people just want to get on with their lives. I'm just some guy who builds hospital wings. No special talent required there."

She moved closer to the counter. "You're wrong. It does take talent to coordinate a project that size. We're talking about adding on a hospital wing that's going to cost a hundred million dollars. I can't even comprehend that much money, but you're going to make it happen." Kelly felt the corners of her mouth turn up in a slight smile. "I have trouble keeping my checkbook balanced."

He grinned. "Me, too. I give it to my bookkeeper

and he does it for me.'' He patted the stool next to him. ''Have a seat.''

She hesitated, then took her glass of wine with her as she circled around the counter. When she'd settled in place, he faced her.

''I'd like to hear about what happened to you. If you were just seventeen, you were probably still in high school when you got pregnant, right?''

Kelly drew in a deep breath. Something about Tanner made her want to share her past. Maybe it was the way he studied her face so intently, or the kindness in his eyes. Maybe it was nothing more than the desire to unburden herself to someone willing to listen. Whatever the reason, she found herself needing to talk.

''I grew up in a small town in Kansas,'' she began. ''My mom died when I was born and my dad raised me by himself.'' Pictures from her past appeared in her brain and made her smile. ''He's a good man and a great father. I always felt as if I were the center of his universe.''

''I hope I can do that for Lia,'' Tanner said.

Kelly studied him. ''I think you will. The fact that you're worried about it means it's all the more likely to happen.'' She paused. ''My dad's a Baptist minister. He has a huge church and the members keep him busy, but he always made time for me.''

She touched the base of her wine glass, but didn't lift it to drink. ''I was a normal kid. I did well in school and I'd always wanted to be a doctor. There wasn't a lot of extra money so I'd planned on getting a scholarship. I did the usual things in high school. There were ups and downs, but whatever happened, however badly I was feeling, I knew I could always go to my dad and tell him. All I had to do was look into his eyes and see the light of his love shining out. That light—his love really—gave me the strength I needed to do the right thing.''

Tanner's warm hand settled over her own. The heat of him and the pressure of his strong fingers nearly distracted her from her story. She had to force herself to remember what she'd been saying.

"In my senior year of high school I fell in love for the first time.''

"I'll bet you were the prettiest girl in school and all the boys wanted you desperately.''

His compliment made her smile. "Not exactly. I'm five ten and I achieved my full height by the time I was thirteen. It took them a while to catch up. But they finally did. Anyway, the night of the homecoming dance, one thing led to another and in the front of Bobby's car, I lost my virginity and got pregnant. It was a full evening.''

This time she did take a sip of her wine, but she used her right hand to hold the glass. She didn't want to pull her left one away from Tanner's touch. Contact with him gave her strength and a feeling of support, which was silly because they were just friends.

She squeezed her eyes shut for a second because nothing made sense anymore. Why did it seem like things had just changed between them?

"You don't have to finish the story if you don't want to,'' he told her.

"Thanks, but there's not much more to tell. I ignored the truth for as long as I could. I think I figured if I ignored it, it would go away. Of course life and pregnancies don't work that way. Then I received word that I'd earned a full scholarship to college. All I had to do was keep my grades up my last semester.''

"No pressure there," Tanner said.

Kelly nodded. "I didn't know what to do or where to turn. Finally I knew I'd have to tell my dad. Somewhere between breakfast and presents Christmas morning I confessed all and broke my father's heart.'' She withdrew her hand from Tanner's grasp and laced her fingers together on her lap.

"He was the best," she said softly, not looking at him, barely allowing herself to remember that time. But it was so hard not to get lost in the past, in the pain of that day and the days that followed.

"He went to the school district and made arrangements for me to finish my classes, even though there was an unwritten policy against pregnant teenagers attending regular classes. He dealt with the parishioners who thought I should be punished. He took me to the doctor, made sure I ate right, and when the time came, he helped me pick out the parents who adopted my child.''

"But?" Tanner probed gently.

"But the light in his eyes had died," she whispered. She drew in a deep breath and risked glancing at him. "I never saw it again. The one thing that told me I was perfect and loved unconditionally was gone. And no matter what I've done since, it's never come back.''

She rose to her feet because it had suddenly become impossible to stay seated. After crossing to the sink, she pressed her hands against the cool porcelain and bowed her head.

"That was the hardest seven months of my life.

At school, no one would talk to me. My boyfriend disappeared the second I told him I was pregnant and my friends were too embarrassed or too angry to have anything to do with me. Going to church was a nightmare. Most of the congregation understood but the ones who judged me were also the most vocal. And I wondered. Was I doing the right thing? After all I was smart and motivated. Maybe I should forget the idea of being a doctor and get a job instead.''

"But you didn't."

"No. We found a nice couple who desperately wanted a child. So I gave her up."

She heard Tanner swear under his breath. "You had a girl?"

She nodded. "Annie Jane. I had an easy delivery, but they wouldn't let me hold her. Instead they took her away and all I could do was wonder if I'd done the right thing, or the easy thing."

Feelings welled up inside of her. Pain at the past, regrets for what she'd done, and what she'd not done. It was too late, she reminded herself. Choices had been made and they couldn't be unmade.

"I've never had any contact with her or her parents, but her grandparents on her adoptive mother's side have stayed in touch with me. They keep me updated on her progress, send pictures. Their daughter couldn't have children, so they're very grateful to me for giving them Annie."

"Does she know she's adopted?" he asked.

"Oh, yes. It hasn't been a secret. But she's not interested in meeting me. Maybe in time, but for now she's happy with her family the way it is." She straightened. "I know she's fine. I know that her life is a good one and that she has loving parents. But I can't help wondering how it all would have been if I hadn't chosen to be selfish. If I'd just—''

She hadn't heard Tanner move, but suddenly he was standing behind her, turning her to face him. ''Don't,'' he commanded. ''Don't say it and don't you dare even think it. You were seventeen years old, Kelly. You had a hell of a choice to make and you did the best you could. Sure you could have kept her and then what? Gotten a job right out of high school? What about your dream of being a doctor?''

''What about my daughter?''

''What about her? Are you saying you could have done better?''

''I don't know.''

His blue eyes darkened as he gripped her shoulders. ''I want to shake you,'' he said. ''Don't do this to yourself. Don't second-guess the past. You have a wonderful life and so does she. If the situation were to happen today, you would have chosen differently. But it wasn't today. You were a kid. Give yourself a break.''

''I want to,'' she said. And she did. She'd spent so much of her life beating herself up for her choices back then. Was it wrong to let the past go? She wanted to believe she was allowed, but she wasn't sure. ''As for my life being wonderful, sometimes it is, but sometimes it's very lonely.''

Tanner's mouth tightened. ''Why did I know you were going to say that?'' he asked, but he didn't seem to be expecting an answer. Instead of holding her shoulders, his hands were moving up and down her arms. ''I wish you hadn't told me this,'' he said, then shook his head when he saw the look on her face. "Don't get all weird on me. I don't mean because I think less of you. If anything, I admire you even more. But knowing about your past makes you..."

"What?"

"Approachable."

He was standing so close, she thought. She could feel his heat warming her. His hands were firm on her arms. He was a strong, solid man—the kind of man who made women feel safe and protected.

"It's as if you're just like everyone else," he murmured.

"I always have been."

"Not to me, and I think I preferred it that way."

"Why?"

"Because it would have kept me from doing this."

She knew what he was going to do before he did it. Even so, his kiss startled her. Not the fact that his lips pressed against hers, but because they felt so right in doing so. There was a sense of coming home—which was crazy, but true. The scent of his body filled her and it was as if she'd already known that scent. He kissed slowly, as if they had all the time in the world. As if taking that time would only increase their passion. Desire flickered low in her belly as heat poured through her body.

He drew his arms around her and pulled her close. She went willingly—practically melting into him— as her arms encircled his neck.

They were nearly the same height but he was so powerfully built that she felt small by comparison. Her breasts nestled easily against his chest and her hips seemed to surge against him with a will of their own. But all that faded when compared to the perfection that was their kiss.

He brushed her mouth gently with his, moving back and forth so slowly that she could have escaped at any time—if she'd wanted to. But what woman would want to move away from the wonder that was Tanner Malone?

She felt the faintest rub of stubble against her chin. The friction delighted her, making her want to feel that slight scratchiness all over her body. Delicious images filled her mind, of them together like this, only more together. Pressed hard and naked, surging in the most intimate dance of all. She was over-heated and breathless and all they'd done was kiss. Good grief, what would happen to her if they actually did make love? She would never survive.

But it would be a glorious way to go.

He drew his tongue along the seam of her mouth. The sensual movement drew her back to the present, to their kiss. She slipped one hand up so that her fingers could bury themselves in his thick, dark hair. Her other hand moved down his back feeling the movement of muscles against her palm. Then she parted her lips and invited him inside.

The jolt when his tongue touched hers nearly made her scream. There was a flash of heat and energy, but that wasn't what aroused her the most. It was Tanner's reaction to their shared intimacy. Beneath the hand on his back she felt his entire body tense. Strength turned to rock. At the same time, he took a step closer and pressed himself against her fully. She felt the length and breadth of his arousal…and it was as impressive as the rest of him.

Kelly found herself getting lost in the experience of kissing him. She clung to him, wanting to be closer. His tongue moved against hers, then explored her mouth. Each caress brought with it new and exciting sensations. She found herself needing more, kissing him back, wanting more. She was thirty-two years old and she couldn't remember the last time a man had *really* kissed her. It was a sad statement on her life.

But it wasn't just being with a man that reduced her legs to jelly. It was specifically this man. Because she'd been on the occasional date and those men had sometimes given her a chaste good-night kiss. Not once had she ever reacted so strongly.

She wanted him and it felt so good to want a man. She wanted to tell him that it was okay with her if he pushed her up against the counter, pulled down her jeans and panties and did it with her right there in the kitchen. She who had never been daring enough to leave the lights on.

His hands moved from her back to her face. He cupped her cheeks as if he were afraid she would try to run away. Had she been able to speak, she would have told him there was nowhere else she would rather be.

He nipped at her lower lip, then soothed the erotic ache with his tongue. He drew her lip into his mouth, sucking her and creating tiny pulls that tugged all the way to her breasts. Her nipples were hard and as hungry as the rest of her.

"Kelly," he breathed against her mouth, then slipped one hand under her braid.

He kissed her again, deeply, and she welcomed him. They circled each other, stroking, learning, breathing heavily. She was so incredibly aroused. Shudders rippled through her as if they'd been kissing for hours. Maybe they had. Maybe the rest of the world had disappeared and only they were left to live in the magic of this moment.

Boldly, she let her hands trail down his back to the high, tight curve of his rear. As if reading her intent, he surged against her, rubbing his arousal against her belly, making her gasp. One of his hands dropped to her waist, then moved up her side toward her breasts.

In the back of her mind a voice whispered that things were getting out of hand and wouldn't that be nice. She caught her breath as his fingers moved higher and higher, reaching for her aching curves. Then her side vibrated.

Tanner wrapped his arms around her and rested his forehead against hers. "I would like to take credit for that, but I'm not good enough."

She smiled faintly, still caught up in what had, until this second, been going on between them. "Too bad," she murmured as she removed her pager and stared at the display. "It's the hospital. I'm guessing it's one of my patients."

He stepped back and motioned to the phone. Kelly picked up the receiver and dialed from memory. Her head was still thick with passion and she was afraid her voice would sound funny. She cleared her throat a couple of times before the nurse's station picked up.

"This is Dr. Hall. I received a page."

"Yes, Doctor. One of your ladies is here. Her name is Wendy…"

The nurse continued talking and Kelly carefully

wrote everything down, but it was incredibly hard to concentrate because Tanner had come up behind her and was trailing damp kisses down the nape of her neck. It was all she could do to keep taking notes. Finally she hung up the phone.

"You have a patient in labor," he said, still standing behind her. He wrapped his arms around her waist and pulled her against his chest. "You have to go."

"Yes," she said as she placed her hands on top of his. Had they really just shared the most extraordinary kiss?

She turned to look at him. Passion darkened his eyes to the color of sapphires. His expression was equal parts aroused and self-satisfied.

"You're something of a kisser, Dr. Hall," he said.

"I could say the same about you."

"Go ahead."

She laughed. "You're a great kisser, Mr. Malone. Thank you."

They were standing close together, but not touching. Then Tanner cupped her face. "I'm not sorry. The timing is probably poor, but I can't regret kissing you."

Kelly drew in a deep breath. With his words, reality crashed in around her. Who they were—why they were together. This wasn't a date and they weren't a couple. She was helping out a friend, nothing more. She didn't do relationships, and Tanner, well, she didn't know all that much about him except that he was in the middle of a hundred-million dollar construction job and had just brought an infant into his life.

She took a step back. "I agree with both sentiments," she said. "The timing is less than perfect. Everything about your life is changing and the last thing you need right now is a woman getting in the way."

"That's my excuse, what's yours?"

Kelly didn't really have one except she'd fallen in the habit of being alone. Right now she couldn't think why.

"I would like to help you with Lia, but it will get complicated if we're more than friends," she said.

She held her breath, then relaxed when he seemed to accept her explanation.

"So now what?" he asked, shoving his hands into his rear pockets. She tried not to notice how the action pulled the material of his jeans tight. Thank goodness she'd been paged. If not, they might have acted out her fantasy of doing it in the kitchen.

"Now we agree to keep it simple. Friends. Good friends."

"I get the message. No more kissing." His mouth tightened. "But I'll be thinking about it, Kelly. Probably for longer than I should."

She swallowed. "Yeah. Me, too. I've got to go."

She collected her purse and walked out of the house. When she got in her car, she found her gaze drawn back to the front door. What would it be like to know that after she'd safely delivered her patient's baby she would be returning here? Not just as Tanner's friend, but as someone important to him.

She didn't have any answers, she told herself as she backed out of the driveway. Nor were they necessary. For now she and Tanner would keep things simple—they would be friends. In time…

Here Kelly wasn't so sure. In time, what? Maybe she would have to figure out why she'd spent all her adult life running from relationships. Maybe she could figure out what was wrong with her. As a child and a teenager, she'd always planned on getting married and having a family. What had happened to that dream? Was it too late to get it back or was she destined to spend the rest of her life alone?

"Tell me good news, Angel," Tanner said as his foreman slumped into the opposite chair.

"It's all good, boss," the short, stocky man said with a grin. He gestured with his unlit cigar. "We're sticking to your revised schedule, so we're catching up a little each week. I've been calling suppliers, and for once they're getting it right. If this keeps up, we'll coast right up to our deadline. Oh, and the toilet problem is fixed."

Tanner let out the breath he'd been holding. For a while he hadn't been sure they were going to come in on time, let alone on budget. Having the funding pulled when he was more than a third of the way through the project had about done him in. Between having to pay for labor and delivered supplies while trying to stall other orders, he'd been within days of going under.

He leaned back in his chair. The situation had been unavoidable, he reminded himself. He paid for many of his materials up front. Suppliers gave him a discount that way, and that discount had been figured into his bid on the project. Labor costs were paid as incurred. Most large projects required loans to float the costs of building until the general contractor was paid, but this time Tanner had decided to use his own money. He had enough, as long as the regular funding came through. Who could have predicted that one of the executives would embezzle the foundation's money?

"It's April now," Angel was saying. "Exterior painting will start in late May or early June, just like we planned. The inside work is going faster than expected." He held up a hand before Tanner could interrupt. "Every department is making sure there are inspections and quality checks every step of the way. No one is going to shortcut on this project."

"Good, because you know the rule." Tanner made a practice of firing any individual or company who cut corners. Everything was built to code, with the finest materials available.

Angel grabbed his clipboard and stood up. "That's it, boss. Now I'm gonna go explain to the electrical contractor that hospitals need a lot of plugs. They're saying we made a mistake in the design. No one needs that many plugs in each room. Not to worry. I know the design's right and by the time I'm done with them, they're gonna know it, too."

He gave a wave and stomped out of the room. Tanner grinned. Angel might not be the most refined guy in the world, but he got the job done.

Tanner was about to turn on his computer and start checking scheduling, when someone else walked into his office. He glanced up and saw his brother Ryan.

"How's life?" Ryan asked as he settled into the chair Angel had vacated. "Did you get much sleep this weekend?"

"More than I thought. Lia wakes up every few hours, but then she goes right back to sleep. The baby nurse Ronni recommended is great. She calls me every couple of hours just to let me know that things are going well at home."

"Sounds like you have it under control."

Tanner nodded. "Here, too, Ryan. I know you've been worried, but the project is on schedule. We'll be meeting the September first date."

Some of the tension in his brother's face eased. Tanner knew that Ryan tried not to show that he was concerned, but Ryan had a lot of responsibility. He was the one who had found the funding for the hospital project, then he'd been the one to recommend Tanner's company. While the temporary loss of funding hadn't been Ryan's fault, he'd taken it hard. He'd busted his butt to get the project up and running, and so far they were doing fine.

"I knew I could count on you," Ryan said.

"You can also count on me to take the kids when you and Ronni head off to get married at the end of the month. I can handle them and Lia, too."

Ryan laughed. "Yeah, right. In your dreams. Your daughter is sleeping her life away right now but that changes. Besides, we've already made other arrangements. My three are going to be well looked after."

"If you're sure," Tanner said. "I'll be happy to take them."

"Worry about your own, right now." Ryan rose and shook his brother's hand. "Congratulations again. Both on the project and on Lia."

"Thanks."

Tanner watched his brother leave, but instead of

returning his attention to his computer, he rose and crossed to the window. His temporary office was going to eventually be the lab. Right now scaffolding obscured most of the view, but he could see out. It was a sunny spring day, with temperatures near sixty. But he didn't see the newly budding flowers planted on the hospital grounds. Instead he pictured his daughter sleeping peacefully in her crib.

He was flying by the seat of his pants with her— which was what he'd done with most of his life. When he'd bought the business, he'd been afraid he would fail completely and publicly, but he hadn't— despite his history of screwing up.

Maybe he was maturing. It was bound to happen eventually. His business was successful and so far fatherhood was even better than he'd thought it would be. He loved Lia, and he was willing to do whatever he had to so that he could give her a decent life.

Thinking of Lia made him think of Kelly because for some reason they were linked together in his brain. And thinking of Kelly made him remember the kiss they'd shared last Sunday. The kiss he hadn't been able to forget.

He was done screwing up, he reminded himself. Which meant no more weekend flings with women like Lucy Ames. He had to go for someone right, or not bother. When he'd first decided to take Lia, he'd told himself he wasn't going to do the relationship thing at all. That would be easier. But now he wasn't so sure. He might be willing to give it a try if it meant being with someone special…someone like Kelly.

Chapter Eight

"So how's my favorite girl in the world?"

Kelly leaned back in her chair and smiled. "I'm great, Dad. How are you?"

"Not bad for an old man."

Kelly shifted the phone so it nestled between her shoulder and her ear, then slipped off her pumps. She'd spent most of the day on her feet. For once she hadn't been interrupted by one of her patients giving birth, so she'd actually gotten through her regular appointments. Now it was nearly six and the office was quiet.

"You're not old. You're just getting started."

"I like to think so," Daniel Hall answered. "But some mornings it's tough to pull on my sweats and go jogging. The boys are starting to beat me."

"I don't believe that."

Her father was as fit today as he had been when

she'd been a little girl. He ran every morning with the high school athletes. Some of them were members of his church, but most weren't. Daniel had been a fixture on the morning exercise scene through hundreds of students' lives. He was always available to listen, or even give advice if asked. More than one crisis had been averted because the kids involved had gone to Daniel. Somehow a man out jogging and sweating wasn't nearly as scary as approaching a minister of a church.

"Tell me what's going on in your life," her father said. "I know you're keeping busy."

"Of course. It comes with the job." She told him a little about work, then brought him up to date on the situation with Tanner and Lia.

Daniel chuckled. "A newborn in the house and a girl at that. I can relate to his shock. You weren't at all what I expected. You were pretty enough, but those diapers. I always wondered how something so small and sweet could produce something so nasty."

"Oh, Dad. You need to let the diaper thing go."

"I can't. I'm scarred for life."

She grinned. "I think Tanner is going to be as well. He's still getting used to the challenges and the responsibility. Lia is a sweet baby, but it's changed everything for him. He's involved with a huge construction project at the hospital and now he's got a daughter."

"He's going to find that she's the greatest joy of his life," he said. "Just like you're mine."

"Thanks." As always, his loving support made her feel safe inside. Even if her father had stopped being proud of her when she'd gotten pregnant, she never doubted that he loved her.

"So," Daniel said. "Tell me about this Tanner Malone. He sounds like a decent guy. Is he cute?"

"Oh, Dad."

"That's twice you've 'oh Da-ad' me in one conversation. What am I doing wrong?"

"Nothing. It's just that you're matchmaking and it's not like that between Tanner and myself." She forced herself *not* to think of the kiss they'd shared over a week ago. Despite the fact that memories of it haunted her nights…not to mention her days.

"So there's no spark between you two? Is spark the right word or am I dating myself?"

"No one says spark much anymore," she said, then tried to figure out how to answer the question without actually lying. "As for Tanner and me, we're just friends. Neither of us are in a place where we'd be comfortable having a relationship. He has a new baby and his work and I'm always swamped with my practice."

There was a long pause, then her father sighed. Kelly's hand tightened on the receiver. She hated that sigh—she knew it meant she'd disappointed her father in some way.

"Dad?"

"I don't understand why you're still hiding," he said at last. "When you were younger and medical school kept you busy, I thought things would change in time. You've done so well. How can I not be proud of you? But you've been in practice for three years. Other doctors manage to find time to have a life. Why not you? Why are you making excuses?"

"It's not like that," Kelly said, stumbling over the words. Hiding? Is that what her father thought?

"Maybe it's not surprising," Daniel went on to

say. "After all you grew up without a mother, but more importantly, you grew up without being able to see a loving marriage first hand. I worried about that, and many times I thought it would be better if I remarried. Except I could never find someone I loved as much as I had loved your mother."

"Daddy, you did a great job," she told him. "No daughter could have asked for a better father. I never missed having a mother because you were always there for me." It was true. When there were awkward "girl" things to discuss, her father had always sensed her needs and had one of their family friends take her out to lunch so she could talk.

"I hope that's true," he said. "But I wish you could have seen the two of us together. Loving her changed my life. It changed me. I was a better person when I was with her. She was the light of my life—my other half and I still miss her."

"I know you do."

"Do you? You've heard me talk, but you have no memories of your mother. I want so much for you, Kelly. I want you to be happy in your work, but I also want you to be happy in your personal life. You don't have to sacrifice everything all the time. Sometimes it's okay just to be."

"I'm fine," she insisted, trying not to think about her small, sterile apartment or the fact that she hadn't been on a date in several years.

"If you're sure, then I won't interfere. I love you, Kelly. I hope you know that. I just want what's best for you."

"I know, Dad. I love you, too."

"Call me in a few days?"

"I promise. Bye."

She hung up the phone. But it was a long time before she collected her purse and left the office. All the way to her car and even as she drove out of the empty parking lot, she thought about what her father had said to her. That she was hiding.

Was he right? Is that what she'd been doing all these years? Thinking about it, she could see that it was a hard habit to break. She'd been determined to maintain her grades when she'd started college. As a pre-med, bio-chemistry major, there hadn't been much time for anything except studying. That first year of school, when everyone else had been making friends and joining clubs, Kelly had buried herself in her books. When she did surface, it was to deal with the guilt of having given up her daughter.

The past returned and with it the moment when she'd told her father that she was pregnant, and then had watched the light go out of his eyes. No matter how hard she'd studied or what she'd achieved later, she'd never been able to make the light come back. When she'd finally realized it never would, it had been the only time in her life when she'd wanted to die.

Kelly drew in a deep breath. Part of the reason she'd worked so hard had been because of her father, but the rest of it had been because of her daughter. It was as if she had to keep proving that her decision to give up Annie Jane was the right one. If she turned out to be a good doctor, then her daughter would understand why she'd made the choice she had. Except deep in her heart Kelly still believed she'd taken the easy way out.

Despite what her father had said all those years ago and despite what Tanner had told her last weekend, she knew they could have made it. Oh, their lives might not have been full of material things. She would have had a baby and been working while going to school part-time. But they would have survived. At least then she wouldn't always wonder how it could have been.

As she wondered now. Except all the wondering in the world didn't change the past. She'd made her choice and there was no going back.

So why was she still hiding?

Her father's question returned to her. She knew there was truth in his words. Was it because she hadn't paid her debt? Was it fear or simply habit? And if she accepted that she was hiding, how much of life had already passed her by? It was too late to change the past, but could she still change her future?

"Now I'm happy to stay a little longer," Gabby Dawson told Tanner as she slipped on her coat. "Your Lia is about the best baby I've ever seen. So sweet and those pretty eyes. Just like yours. She's going to be a beauty when she grows up."

"Tell me about it. I'm going to have to get a really big stick to scare off all the boys in the neighborhood." Tanner glanced down at the sleeping infant. "We'll just start calling you 'Trouble' as soon as you hit fourteen. How does that sound, little girl?"

Lia slept on, oblivious of being the subject of conversation.

"We'll be fine," he told Gabby.

"All right then. I'll be off. Same time tomorrow, right?"

"Absolutely."

The doorbell rang. "I'll get that on my way out," Gabby called as she headed for the stairs. "You have a nice evening, Tanner."

"I will," he said as he followed her into the living room. Despite her fifty-something years, she moved with quick grace. She was a whiz with Lia, and Tanner was grateful Ronni had recommended her. Until his daughter was old enough to come to the office with him, or attend regular daycare, he could rest easy with nurse Gabby in charge.

"It's Dr. Hall," Gabby said as she pulled open the front door. "I was just leaving," she told Kelly. "Lia has been an angel. I doubt she'll give you a minute's trouble. Now you two have a nice night."

She gave a quick wave and was gone.

Kelly stared after her. "She reminds me of Robin Williams in that movie *Mrs. Doubtfire,* although she's a lot prettier."

"And she doesn't have the accent. So you think my baby nurse is a cross-dresser?"

Kelly laughed. "No, that's not what I meant. She's just a warm, caring person, like that character." She set her purse on the small table by the front door. "How was your day?"

"Good." But not as good as she looked, he thought.

Tanner had to shove his hands into his pockets to keep from walking over to her and pulling her into his arms. She wore a navy suit with a silky pink blouse. High heels made her legs look even longer than usual. She'd pulled her hair back into a fancy twist. From head to toe, she was a class act.

He on the other hand, had barely walked in the

door fifteen minutes ago. He hadn't even had a chance to shower.

"What?" she asked. "You're staring at me. Do I have ink on my nose or something?"

"Not at all. I was just noticing that you look terrific, while I had a close encounter with a paint machine." He turned slowly to show her his paint-splattered back. "We come from two different worlds, that's for sure."

"Is that bad?"

"No. But I've been thinking." He rocked back on his heels. He didn't want to talk about this with her, but he didn't have a choice. "It's been nearly two weeks since Lia was born."

"I know. I was there."

"Yeah, well, you've got a life of your own and I've sort of taken it over. You've been here every night, except when you had to deliver a baby last Friday. You've spent two weekends helping me out. You've been a great friend, but I don't want to take advantage of that."

"You're not. I've been happy to help." She folded her arms over her chest. "You're throwing me out, aren't you?"

Tanner didn't know how to answer. Despite the fact that he was dirty and tired, he still wanted her. He'd wanted her before they'd ever kissed, but now that he'd experienced the passion possible between them, his desire had only increased. She was an incredible woman—everything a man could want. Smart, successful, caring, warm, sexy as hell and completely out of his league.

He'd played the game enough times to know when it was going to work and when it wasn't. Between their differences in career and his status as a new father, he didn't stand a chance with her. Under different circumstances, he might have given it a run anyway, figuring something short-term would be better than nothing at all. Except he wasn't comfortable with that. Not only because of Lia, but because Kelly was someone he cared about and he didn't want to play games with her.

"I'm not throwing you out," he said at last. "You're welcome to stay as long as you'd like. However, I don't want to take advantage of you or cramp your style."

She stared at him. Her hazel brown eyes were wide and clear as she studied him, obviously assessing the truth of his words. "And if I told you I didn't have enough of a personal life to warrant a style?"

"Then I'd ask you if you'd like to have a glass of wine with me."

"Red or white?"

"Whichever you'd prefer."

She smiled. "We could mix them together and make our own special blend."

He shuddered. "No, thank you."

She laughed and led the way to the kitchen. "I think red tonight," she told him as she slid onto one of the stools by the counter.

"Red it is."

He pulled a cabernet from the built-in wine rack, then put it back and drew out a merlot. He held up the bottle, and when she nodded, he started to open it.

"So was that really about me?" she asked. "Are you genuinely concerned about my personal life, or were you thinking of your own? While I don't have a style, I'm guessing yours had been refined by years of practice.''

He set the open wine in front of her and collected two glasses. ''I had one once. I don't anymore.''

''So you've pulled yourself out of the dating game. Are hearts breaking all over Honeygrove?''

''Maybe one or two.''

''Let me guess. Young, beautifully stunning women with aspirations to be models or actresses?''

He wasn't sure if she was teasing or insulting him. ''Attractiveness helps, but it's not the only requirement.''

''And none of them ever convinced you to walk down the aisle?''

''A few tried,'' he admitted as he poured them each a glass of wine. ''But I never wanted that. I'm more the serial monogamy type. It's all I know.''

Her expression turned serious. ''What do you mean?''

''Ryan and I grew up in foster homes. We were considered too old to adopt. Some of the time we were in the same family, but just as often we were split up. It was tough.''

She frowned. ''I can't even imagine. I lived in the same house and slept in the same room until I left for college. In fact, it's still there, now. My dad didn't even turn it into a guest room. Not that he's keeping it as a shrine or anything, but there are already enough spare rooms. I know it's waiting for me whenever I go back to visit.''

''That would have been nice,'' he said as he touched his glass to hers, then took a sip of the wine. ''But Ryan and I moved around a lot. When we were in the same house, we often talked about what it would have been like if our parents hadn't been killed. Ryan could remember more than I could. He wanted to recreate what he'd lost, which is one of the reasons he married Patricia, his first wife. She wanted to make a home and he needed that.''

She looked at him. "But you went in a different direction. Because you didn't know what a normal family life looked like?''

"Maybe.''

"I understand that completely. I mean my father loved me and was always there for me, but it was just the two of us. I never had a mother—she died giving birth to me.''

"Is that why you became an obstetrician? So you could save other women?''

Kelly blinked several times. "I don't think so. I never thought about it that way.'' She shrugged. "It's funny. I talked to my father tonight and he was discussing this very topic. He said he felt badly that I'd never had the experience of watching a loving marriage at work. He thinks that's one of the reasons I'm not married myself.''

"Is it?''

"I don't know that answer, either.''

"I'm not sure watching would have helped,'' he said. "I saw plenty of married couples. Some got along great, but others—'' He shook his head. "They were a disaster.''

"Was Ryan's first marriage happy?''

"It looked that way. At least from the outside. Although their kids are great, so it probably was.'' He leaned against the counter. "You don't have to worry that he's carrying a torch for Patricia. He loved her, but it's been a long time. He's let her go. He thinks the world of Ronni.''

She leaned forward and rested her elbows on the counter. ''Thanks for reassuring me, but I wasn't worried. Ronni's got a good head on her shoulders. I don't think she would have fallen for someone who was still in love with another woman. Ryan's a lucky man—he's getting a wonderful woman.''

Tanner couldn't help wondering why some man hadn't gotten lucky enough to snag Kelly. She was incredible and from what he could tell, completely single. It had to be by choice.

She took another sip of wine. ''You said that your style was serial monogamy, but what do you like in a woman? Aside from her being incredibly beautiful.''

''I'm going to ignore that last comment. I already said that beauty isn't all that important to me.''

''Uh huh.'' She didn't sound the least bit convinced.

Tanner was intrigued by the question. He liked that Kelly wanted to know about his favorite ''type.'' While it wasn't a guarantee that she was interested, it did indicate that she'd given him a little thought.

''What do I like in a woman?'' He grinned. ''You want the absolute truth or the politically correct version?''

''Oh, absolute truth.''

''Can you handle it?''

The corners of her mouth turned up. ''Mr. Malone, if you're attempting to challenge me, do not for a moment underestimate my abilities.''

He leaned forward, resting his forearms on the

PLAY "LUCKY 7" AND GET
THREE FREE GIFTS!

HOW TO PLAY:

1. With a coin, carefully scratch off the silver box at the right. Then check the claim char see what we have for you — **FREE BOOKS** and a gift — **ALL YOURS! ALL FREE!**

2. Send back this card and you'll receive brand-new Silhouette Special Edition® nov These books have a cover price of $4.50 each in the U.S. and $5.25 each in Canada, they are yours to keep absolutely free.

3. There's no catch. You're un no obligation to buy anything. charge nothing — ZERO — your first shipment. And you d have to make any minimum num of purchases — not even one!

4. The fact is thousands of readers enjoy receiving books by mail from the Silhouette Rea Service.™ They enjoy the convenience of home delivery. . . they like getting the best novels at discount prices, BEFORE they're available in stores…and they love their *Hea Heart* newsletter featuring author news, horoscopes, recipes, book reviews and much more

5. We hope that after receiving your free books you'll want to remain a subscriber. the choice is yours — to continue or cancel, any time at all! So why not take us up on invitation, with no risk of any kind. You'll be glad you did!

YOURS FREE!

PLAY LUCKY 7 FOR THIS EXCITING FREE GIFT!

THIS SURPRISE MYSTERY GIFT COULD BE YOURS FREE WHEN YOU PLAY

LUCKY 7!

Visit us on-line at
www.romance.net

The Silhouette Reader Service™ — Here's how it works:

Accepting your 2 free books and gift places you under no obligation to buy anything. You may keep the books and gift and return the shipping statement marked "cancel." If you do not cancel, about a month later we'll send you 6 additional novels and bill you just $3.80 each in the U.S., or $4.21 each in Canada, plus 25¢ delivery per book and applicable taxes if any.* That's the complete price and — compared to cover prices of $4.50 each in the U.S. and $5.25 each in Canada — it's quite a bargain! You may cancel at any time, but if you choose to continue, every month we'll send you 6 more books, which you may either purchase at the discount price or return to us and cancel your subscription.

*Terms and prices subject to change without notice. Sales tax applicable in N.Y. Canadian residents will be charged applicable provincial taxes and GST.

If offer card is missing write to: Silhouette Reader Service, 3010 Walden Ave., P.O. Box 1867, Buffalo, NY 14240-1867

BUSINESS REPLY MAIL
FIRST-CLASS MAIL   PERMIT NO. 717   BUFFALO, NY

POSTAGE WILL BE PAID BY ADDRESSEE

SILHOUETTE READER SERVICE
3010 WALDEN AVE
PO BOX 1867
BUFFALO NY 14240-9952

NO POSTAGE
NECESSARY
IF MAILED
IN THE
UNITED STATES

counter. Their faces were only inches apart. He could see the flecks of gold in her eyes and several tiny freckles on her nose. Her lips were a temptation he warned himself to avoid.

"I like an equal combination of intelligence, humor and trashy lingerie. Leather isn't a requirement, but black or red lace is."

Her well-shaped mouth fell open as her eyes widened in shock. "Oh my."

"You asked."

"So I did." She licked her lips. "And how successful are you at achieving your ideal?"

"The trashy underwear is pretty easy. It's the intelligence and humor that I have trouble with. I'm not in the right profession for women like that to come calling."

"I don't understand."

He straightened. "I'm a contractor," he said bluntly. "I make enough money, but I wear jeans, not suits. Yeah, I have a degree, but I got it going to school at night. Actually I had a scholarship, but I screwed up partying too much my freshman year and got kicked out. I didn't have any skills, so I got a grunt job working for a contractor. Ten years later I had a degree and was a partner. Two year after that, I bought him out and changed the name."

"Impressive."

"Is it?" He shrugged. "I'm just some guy from the wrong side of the tracks. I prefer movies and sports to ballet and opera, although I do like the theater. I like good wine, but I'm not a snob about it. In my opinion beer and potato chips are a perfectly acceptable food group."

"None of that sounds bad to me," she said.

He wanted to believe her. He wanted to think they were doing more than just playing, but he knew that wasn't the case. When Kelly made up her mind to get involved, it would be with another doctor, or a lawyer, or maybe some upper-level corporate executive.

"So tell me about your Mr. Right. He's rich and successful, with a bunch of degrees."

She straightened. "You seem to have more answers than I do. I haven't thought much about Mr. Right, or Mr. Anybody. I don't really date much. Work keeps me busy."

"Not that busy. You're way too pretty and successful not to have a bunch of men hanging around you."

She surprised him by blushing. Color climbed up her cheeks and she looked away. "Yet I remain surprisingly unfettered by men. It's one of life's great mysteries."

I want to change that. But he only thought the words, he didn't say them. Nor did he move closer, even though he wanted to.

The kitchen seemed to shrink in size and all he could think about was taking her in his arms and kissing her. He wanted to feel her next to him again. He wanted her tall, lean body pressed against him, her breasts flattening against his chest. He wanted to get hard and rub his arousal against her belly, then...

"I have to warn you that I'm only yours for the next two weeks," she said. "After that, my time has been committed to someone else."

"I see." He tried to ignore the flare of jealousy burning inside of him. An old boyfriend returning?

"Yes, I'm going to be involved in a rather complex relationship. There will be four of us all together."

He caught the light of laughter in her eyes. "Four of you, huh? Sounds kinky."

"Actually, it's going to be a lot of fun. I'm taking Ryan's kids while he and Ronni run off to get married."

"You are?" They'd asked Kelly?

"Don't sound so surprised. I'll remind you that I've been the one helping you out with Lia. I do know something about children."

"It's not that. I told them I could still do it."

She laughed. "You're incredibly optimistic. Lia isn't going to be sleeping this much forever. In the next week or so, she's going to be awake more and more. You'll have your hands full with one newborn. You don't need three other kids tossed into the mix."

"We could join our forces together," he said impulsively. "You're staying at Ryan's right? I could bring Lia and stay with you. I know my niece and nephews pretty well and they can be a handful."

As he waited for Kelly to answer, he told himself he was being crazy. Even if she wanted him along, they were already spending too much time together. Did he really want to head into this dangerous territory?

"I'd like that," she said.

As she spoke the words, something clicked into place inside of him. He had a bad feeling he was already in too deep and it was too late to think about getting out now. The only course of action left to him was to follow this road to the end. Maybe, for once in his life, he was going to get it right.

Chapter Nine

The Women's Center Clinic took up half the second floor of a small, older office building in downtown Honeygrove. Kelly spent every other Thursday afternoon and evening at the clinic, donating her time. Her office here, with its scarred wooden desk and a cracked window, was a far cry from her spacious suite back at her regular practice, but Kelly didn't mind. Her purpose was to provide quality health care for those who wouldn't otherwise be able to receive it.

"All right, Granny Bea," Kelly said as she patted the older woman's arm. "Those supplements are working. According to the latest test, you have the bones of a seventeen-year-old runner."

The white-haired grandmother grinned at her. "You're exaggerating, Dr. Kelly, and we both know it."

"Maybe a little, but you're doing better. Keep taking those pills. Tell Sharon, the nurse up front, to give you another refill. Be faithful, all right?"

The tiny woman, a little bent but still in good physical condition, rose to her feet. She used a cane to help her balance. "You're a good girl," Granny Bea said. "I appreciate that you worry about me."

"Of course I do. You have my number, right?" Kelly made sure all her clinic patients had her pager number. If there was an emergency, most of them wouldn't bother going to a hospital. Large institutions hadn't been kind to the women in this neighborhood.

Granny Bea patted her purse. "Right behind my driver's license." She chuckled. "Not that I drive anymore, but I figure if I win the lottery one day, I want to be current so I can go right out and buy a big Mercedes. A black one."

"I can't wait to see you behind the wheel."

Granny Bea was still laughing as she walked to the door. "See you in six months, Dr. Kelly. You take care of yourself."

"Granny Bea," Kelly called. "You know the rule."

The elderly lady shook her head. "Silly child. You really think I'm doing anything like that, with my husband gone to his reward nearly ten years ago."

"You never know, Granny Bea. If you win the lottery, you're going to find yourself chasing away young men with your cane. I want you to be prepared."

"I think it's foolish. I only use them for water

balloons with my grandson. Of course he thinks I'm incredibly hip for such an old lady.''

She reached into the large jar of condoms Kelly kept by the door. One of the rules of both her clinic and her private practice was that every patient had to take a handful home. She didn't want anyone telling her she'd gotten pregnant or caught a sexually transmitted disease because she didn't have any handy protection.

"Bye, Granny Bea."

"Bye, child. You take care and find yourself a man one of these days."

Kelly grinned. "Yes, ma'am."

She was still smiling when she walked into the first examining room.

"Hi, Dr. Kelly," Corina said from her seat on the table.

"How are you feeling?"

"Fat." Corina wrinkled her nose. "I can't believe how huge I am."

"Hey, you're eight months pregnant. What did you expect?"

"I'm the size of the space shuttle."

Kelly studied the seventeen year old's round belly. "Generally women don't make space shuttle size until their ninth month. You're more like the nose cone."

"Very funny."

"I am," Kelly agreed cheerfully. "How are you feeling otherwise?"

While Corina told of swelling and the occasional aches and pains of a basically textbook pregnancy, Kelly examined her. Unfortunately Corina hadn't become a patient until after she was pregnant, so the free condoms hadn't been available in time. Now this pretty, intelligent young woman faced motherhood the month she was supposed to be graduating from high school.

"Tell me what you're eating," Kelly said.

Corina rolled her eyes. "Three servings of protein, one with each meal. Milk with every meal. Fresh vegetables, four servings and at least two fruits. No sodas, only one candy bar every couple of days."

"You're still getting the food stamps?"

Corina nodded. Her long black braids swayed with the movement. She had beautiful wide, brown eyes and skin the color of cafe au lait.

"I keep them at a friend's house," Corina said. "And I only shop for a couple of days at a time. My mom doesn't know about them."

"Good."

The teenager's mother had a drug problem, not to mention a fondness for alcohol. There wasn't much money left over for things like food and heat. Until Kelly had stepped in, Corina had often gone without a decent meal for days at a time.

"How's school?" Kelly asked.

"Okay. I'm studying hard. I've been talking to my teachers about maybe taking my finals early, so that I don't miss them. The baby's due that week."

"I'm glad you're planning ahead, but you do know that the baby might be late, right? This is your first and they like to take their time."

"I know. I just want to be prepared." Corina's chin dropped. "I'm thinking of getting a job when I graduate."

"For the summer, you mean?"

"Not exactly."

Kelly's heart froze. As the teenager continued to avoid looking at her, her concern grew. "I thought you were going to college in the fall. You have that scholarship to Stanford. Corina, that's an incredible opportunity. You're one of the smartest young women I've ever met. You have a chance to be anything you want. Why would you turn your back on that?"

The girl shrugged. "I wouldn't, exactly."

"Then what's going on?"

Corina shrugged again.

Kelly struggled for patience. "If you stay here, you'll always be trapped by your past. Look around you. Is this what you want for yourself? Your mother has been on drugs since she was twelve. You don't know who your father is. You have half brothers and sisters scattered who knows where. When you leave this town, you can be anyone you want. Your past stops here and you only have to worry about your future. You have dreams, I know you do. We've talked about them. Why don't you want the chance to make them come true?"

Corina blinked back tears. "I want that so much," she whispered. "But it's not like you think. All my friends...they keep their babies. They stay here and find a life. They've been telling me that I'm a bad person for wanting to give up my baby. Half of them won't even speak to me anymore. They're saying if I was a real woman, I couldn't give up my child, and that I'm selfish and wrong."

Tears flowed in earnest now. Corina brushed them away. "Dr. Kelly, I want to be just like you. I want to go to medical school and make something of myself, then I want to come back to a place like this and save people's lives. I can't do that with a baby. I can't. I want to go to college, but now I'm afraid that it's wrong to want so much. Maybe they're right. Maybe I should stay here and just get a job. Maybe learn to do hair or something.''

For Kelly, listening to Corina was like staring into the mirror of her own past. She wasn't sure what to think, let alone say.

''Dr. Kelly? You have to tell me what to do.''

Kelly pressed her lips together. Who was she to give answers? She'd messed up her own life so much she hadn't been on a date in years. She was afraid to allow herself any joy because she felt she didn't deserve it. According to her father, she was hiding behind a busy schedule. And she suspected he was right.

She knew the past had a way of catching up with a person, but she hadn't expected it to come in the form of a lost, frightened seventeen year old.

Kelly opened her mouth to speak, but she couldn't find any words. Just then her pager went off. Grateful for the interruption, she glanced down at the display.

''It's the hospital,'' she said, trying to keep the relief out of her voice. ''I have to call them.''

When she made the call, she was told about an emergency with one of her patients. She hurried back into the examining room.

''I have to go,'' she said, telling herself there was no need to feel guilty. ''Make an appointment for two weeks and we'll talk then, all right?''

Corina was still crying.

''I'm sorry,'' Kelly said. ''It's an emergency. Remind Sharon to give you your vitamins. You're doing great. Hang in there.''

What pitiful advice, Kelly thought as she ran down the stairs and raced toward her car. The worst thing Corina could do was to be like her.

As she drove toward the hospital, Kelly vowed she would make it up to the girl. Just as soon as she figured out how.

Tanner felt as if he'd stumbled into an old master's painting. Kelly sat in the rocking chair in the corner, holding Lia in her arms. Subtle light brought out the gold in Kelly's blond hair and made her skin glow. Lia was awake and staring up into Kelly's eyes.

Mother and child, he thought as he continued to study them. A month ago he couldn't have imagined having either of them in his life. Now he didn't know what his world would be like without them.

Kelly looked up at him. ''You're not working,'' she said. ''The wallpaper isn't going to hang itself. Or are you waiting for me to offer.''

''No, I'll do it.''

She smiled and some of his tension eased. When Kelly had first arrived a couple of hours before, she'd been quiet and withdrawn. Normally she enjoyed talking about her day, but this time all she'd said was that she'd had an emergency at the hospital and that it had cut into her time at the clinic. She'd gone back to see as many patients as possible, but some hadn't been able to wait for her.

Tanner knew there was something else bothering her, but he wasn't going to pry. When she wanted to talk, he would listen. Until then, he was content to enjoy her company.

He checked the back of the border print he held. It was tacky but not too wet, so he climbed the short ladder and carefully smoothed it into place.

"It's crooked," Kelly said helpfully. "And there are about a dozen air pockets."

"Thanks," he muttered, reaching up to adjust the paper. But he'd waited too long and it didn't slide against the wall anymore. He gave a hard shove. Instead of moving, the border print tore. A short piece separated from the rest and fluttered to the floor.

"Don't say anything," he commanded as he ripped off the rest of the strip and flung it down. "I hate hanging wallpaper."

Kelly clear her throat. "Wow, so when you offered to pay me back by wallpapering my house, you were lying. Even I can do better than you."

"Yeah, well, I hate hanging wallpaper. Why can't people just use paint?" He hunched his shoulder and turned to glare at her. "I wasn't lying. I would have done it. I was just hoping you'd let me do something else. Maybe something simple like re-wiring your house."

"Or you could have one of your men do it."

He shook his head. "That wouldn't work. It's my debt, so I have to pay you back."

"No debt," she said softly. "We're friends, Tanner. I'm happy to help."

She was tall and athletic, not at all petite or dainty, yet she was the most feminine woman he'd ever known. The hands holding his daughter were strong and capable. She was someone he could de-

pend on and there hadn't been many types like that
in his life.

"I can't believe I'm doing this," he said, snag-
ging one of the fallen strips of border print.

"Hanging paper?"

"No, hanging a print that's ballerina teddy bears.
It's so girly."

Kelly laughed. "You have a daughter. Get used
to the girl thing."

"I guess. I even ordered curtains and the matching lamp. The good news is that when I told Lia
about it, she was really happy."

"Oh? How did you know this?"

"She smiled at me." He made the statement
faintly defensively, but he knew that she'd been
smiling at him. Her lips had curved and everything.

"Tanner, she's three weeks old. She can't smile.
It was gas."

"It was not."

"Right." Her look and her tone were indulgent.

He shifted his attention to his daughter. Three
weeks. Is that all the time it had been? It felt longer.

"She still doesn't have any toys," he said. "I
have to find time to get some."

Kelly shifted Lia and crossed her legs. "Speaking
of buying things for your daughter, I've been thinking about throwing you a baby shower."

"Why?"

She grinned. "Don't look so panicked. It won't
hurt…much. Actually the shower isn't for you, it's
for Lia. So many people want to see her, and probably see her with you. It would be a lot of fun. We
could register you at the baby store and at a toy
store. What do you think?"

"Why?"

"You keep asking that. It's a girl thing. Trust me. I'll take care of everything. Just say yes."

He had a bad feeling he was going to regret it, but he muttered, "Yes," then asked if anything strange happened at baby showers.

"Define strange," she told him.

"Never mind."

"We'll need to pick a date so that I can mail out invitations. We can't do it for her one month birthday. For one thing, that's next weekend and I can't plan that fast. Not to mention next weekend is booked. I'll have Ryan's kids until Sunday evening. Maybe we can celebrate her six week birthday."

"Whatever." He began measuring out a length of the border print. At least he'd remembered to buy double the amount so that he would have enough, despite the occasional mishap. "I can't believe you're taking Ryan's three kids for the weekend."

"I tried to take just a couple of them, but he got pretty insistent that I take all or none. What a perfectionist he is."

He glanced at her. Laughter glittered in her eyes. "You're nothing like I thought you'd be," he told her.

"Meaning?"

"You have a sense of humor. You're human. I thought doctors were stuffy by nature."

"They try to teach us that, but I never had time to fit that particular class into my schedule."

"It's not just that," he said. "You don't act like you're God. You treat people with respect. I thought you'd disapprove of what I do for a living."

She straightened in the rocking chair and stared

at him. "How could you think that? Tanner, you're brilliant at what you do. How many people do you know who could coordinate a project of this magnitude? We're not talking about recarpeting a living room. This is a one-hundred million dollar project."

"It's just a building. You save lives."

"And without buildings, people would die from exposure. Everyone contributes in a different way. I would never judge someone based on their work."

"Like I said, you're not how I imagined."

"Doctors are real people too," she said. "If we seem a little crabby at times, it's just because we had to spend so much time in school."

He looked around the room, then his gaze settled on his daughter, now dozing in Kelly's arms. "I never thought I would see anything like this. You sitting there, holding my daughter. Of course I never thought I'd have a child."

"How do you like it?"

"She's the best thing that ever happened to me."

Kelly's smile turned tender. "I'm glad. I'm glad you kept her and I'm glad you two are so happy together."

"Me, too."

He was also glad that Kelly was in his life, but he didn't tell her that. This wasn't the time. Then he wondered if that would ever change. Kelly wasn't for him—even if he was the kind of man who did long-term commitments. Which he didn't. So they would just stay friends and he would make sure that was enough.

Tanner clutched the handle of the baby carrier so hard, he was afraid he might crack the plastic. This was fine, he told himself. There was nothing to worry about. Except he *was* worried.

He stared around the brightly colored waiting area of the medical office. A parade of animals danced across the walls. There were child-sized chairs, as well as those designed for adults, and a collection of toys in the corner. Nothing to fear. So why was there a knot the size of a basketball sitting in the bottom of his stomach?

The office door opened and Kelly walked in. She wore tailored dark slacks and a fitted soft-looking sweater that hugged her curves. The swell of her breasts was nearly enough to take his mind off his panic. Nearly...but not completely.

"Sorry I'm late," she said. "I was running behind with my patients and..." She took one look at him and laughed. "Relax, Tanner. Lia's the one getting the examination, not you."

"I wish it was me," he said glumly. "What if there's something wrong? What if she's sick? What if—"

"Stop!" Kelly said. She took the baby carrier from him and glanced down. As usual, Lia was sound asleep, apparently unaware of her father's concern. Kelly took a seat and patted the cushion next to her.

"You could take a lesson from your daughter," she said. "Now sit down and take a deep breath."

He glared at her, then perched on the edge of the sofa. "You're not taking this seriously."

"Of course I am. Lia is here to see her doctor. She's one month old and it's time for her first well-baby visit. There is every indication that she's a normal, healthy, thriving infant. If there is a problem, better to catch it early. Ronni's a great doctor. You know that.''

"I know.'' He shifted on the sofa. "Sorry. I know I'm acting crazy.''

"You're acting like a worried parent, but in this case, there's no reason to be.''

"You're right.'' He studied her. "Thanks for being here with me. I hadn't really intended for you to take time off work to hold my hand.''

She smiled. "Oh, please. That was exactly your intention. No way you would have survived this on your own.''

The office door opened again and a mother with a young boy walked in. While the woman went to the glass partition at the reception desk to sign them in, the boy walked over and stared at Lia.

"What's her name?'' he asked.

"Lia,'' Tanner told him.

"I'm John.'' He held out his hand. There were several tiny stitches along the side of his index finger and across his palm. "Billy and me were playing with a broken bottle and we got cut. I'm better now, but playing with a broken bottle is bad.''

Kelly smiled at the boy. He couldn't be more than five or six. She scooted forward and stared at the stitches, then pointed to a thin, pale line on her own hand.

"That exact thing happened to me,'' she said. "I was about your age.''

John's brown eyes widened. "Did you have to get stitches, too?''

"I sure did. I cried and cried. I was very sorry I'd ever picked up that piece of glass and I never did it again.''

"I didn't cry," John said. Then he glanced at his mom and shrugged. "Well, I did a little."

Tanner found himself caught up in the conversation. Kelly was so easy and natural with the little boy. It was as if she'd known him for years, instead of just a few minutes. When John's mother came over to collect him, she smiled an apology.

"Sorry. He's a talker."

"He's very sweet," Kelly told the woman.

It made no sense, Tanner thought. Why on earth hadn't some guy snatched Kelly up before now? She was a prize. Not only was she bright and successful, but she had the most giving heart he'd ever seen.

She was different from the kind of woman he usually found himself attracted to. He would bet a month's paycheck that she didn't go for trashy lingerie, nor did she wear much makeup. But he was starting to see the appeal of the natural look, not to mention the fact that thoughts of Kelly in plain cotton had kept him up more than one night.

"What a cutie," Kelly said when John's mother had led him to the other side of the waiting room where they'd started on a puzzle.

"You're great with kids. Why didn't you become a pediatrician?"

She didn't say anything, nor did her body language change, but Tanner could tell she'd shut him out as surely as if she'd started building a brick wall between them.

"What?" he asked. "What's wrong? What did I say?"

"Nothing."

"Kelly, don't. Why are you upset?"

"I'm not."

But her gaze avoided his. Then, before he could pursue the matter, a nurse opened the door leading to the examining rooms. "Lia Malone?"

"That's us," Tanner said. He took the carrier from Kelly and stood up.

"It's just through here," the nurse said. She led them into another brightly colored room, this one with a small examining table and too much medical equipment for Tanner to ever be comfortable. The knot in his stomach doubled in size.

"Hi," Ronni said as she entered. She wore a white coat over scrubs. "Don't say it. I'm a mess. My first appointment of the day threw up on me, and I haven't had time to go home and get a change of clothes. I normally keep a spare set here, but they got thrown up on last week and I haven't brought them back. How's Lia?"

"Great," Tanner said. "I'm sure there's nothing wrong."

"I'm sure, too," Ronni said, her voice reassuring. "I know the first couple of baby visits are nerve-racking on you new parents, but it will get better."

Kelly leaned against the closed door. "Speaking of nerves, how are you holding up?"

Ronni wrinkled her nose. "You mean given the fact that Ryan and I are leaving tomorrow to get married?" She held up her hand to show it was steady. "I'm nervous, but only on the inside. I can't believe we're doing this. I'm incredibly happy and scared. But more happy than scared. I know it's the right thing. I love him and we're going to have a great life together."

"That's what you have to focus on," Kelly said.

"Remember that he's the man you love and you'll be fine."

"Exactly," Ronni said. "Besides, all I have to say is 'I do,' right? How hard can that be?"

The two women laughed, but Tanner didn't join in. He was too busy thinking, once again, that his brother had gotten lucky with the woman he'd chosen. Ronni and Ryan *were* going to have a great life together. Ryan made it look so easy, first with Patricia and now with Ronni. How did he do that? How did he know when it was right? How did he know that it was all okay to commit himself to a particular woman?

Not that it mattered, Tanner told himself. He wasn't the marrying kind. And even if he was, there weren't any likely candidates around.

His gaze settled on Kelly. He already knew that she was a prize. He also knew that she was out of his league. So there was no point in wishing for what he couldn't have.

Words to live by, he told himself. Words he'd repeated more than once. Words that suddenly didn't seem to ring so true.

Chapter Ten

"I can't believe I'm so nervous," Ronni said as she refolded a cream lace and silk nightgown for the third time. "I guess it's because, well, you know."

Kelly and Alex exchanged a look. "I could be wrong," Alex said, her voice teasing, "but it might be because you're getting married. What do you think, Kelly?"

"Sounds like a good reason to me," Kelly told her. "Did you get any sleep at all?"

Ronni sank onto the bed and covered her face with her hands. "No. I was determined to spend last night here." She motioned to the beautifully decorated bedroom of her newly remodeled condo. "I wanted to preserve some traditions, like not seeing the groom too much before the wedding. But I'm so used to staying at the gatehouse at Ryan's that my bed felt unfamiliar. Plus I missed him."

She dropped her hands to her lap. "I guess some of it is because I've never gotten married before. What if I don't like it?"

Kelly rolled her eyes. "You're crazy about the guy and even more crazy about his kids. What's not to like?"

"You're right. I can't imagine not being with him. Ryan is the man I've been waiting for all my life."

"Are you sorry you're not having a big wedding?" Alex asked. She dropped Ronni's makeup bag into the open suitcase on the bed, then settled next to it.

"Absolutely not." Ronni shuddered. "Neither of us wanted the hassle. He's still dealing with the hospital wing, I have my practice. When would we find the time?" She pressed her hand to her stomach. "Not to mention the fact that I'm pregnant."

Kelly leaned back in the chair by the window. "As your doctor, I'm not even sure what to say about that. I carefully hand out condoms at every visit, but did that help? Noooo. I can see I'm going to have to be more detailed with my explanations and inform my patients that it's not enough to have them in the house. Instead, they actually have to be used."

"I know." Ronni hung her head for a second, then glanced up, grinning. "But I can't be sorry. I'm thrilled about the baby."

Kelly turned her attention to Alex. "What about you? Do we have to have this talk?"

Alex raised her hands in a gesture of surrender. "I'm not having sex, so it's not an issue."

"Just remember if you do, safety is important."

"Yes, Mom."

The three women laughed.

Ronni stood up. "I need to finish packing, then check my makeup. Other than that, I think I'm ready." She'd already pinned her bright red hair up into a French twist. Subtle make-up accentuated her green eyes.

"Are you wearing your wedding suit on the plane?" Alex asked.

"No. I'll change there." Ronni walked to the closet and removed a white suit protected by clear plastic. She held it in front of her. "What do you think?"

"It's wonderful," Kelly said as she took in the sophisticated suit with a short skirt and fitted jacket. As much as she teased her friend about being pregnant, the reality was Ronni was only two-and-a-half months along and barely showed. The tailored suit, simple but elegant, would show off her figure perfectly. "Is that as low cut as it looks?"

Faint color stained Ronni cheeks. "Yeah. I thought I'd distract Ryan during the ceremony. You know, in case he's a little nervous."

"A woman with a plan," Alex said. "Very clever."

Ronni carefully placed the suit into her luggage. "I think that's the last of it." She glanced around the room. "Okay, so all that's left is the kids. Are you going to be all right with them, Kelly?"

Kelly grinned. "I swear we'll be fine." She began ticking off points on her fingers. "Drew and Lisbeth are still in school. The baby-sitter will pick them up when they get out, then swing by and get Griffin from day care. She'll stay with them until I get there. My last appointment is at four." Kelly paused to glance at her watch. It was about twelve thirty now. She and Alex had both used their lunch breaks to stop by and wish Ronni luck.

"The sitter can stay late tonight if you get hung up with an emergency," Ronni told her.

"I don't think that's going to happen. This isn't my weekend on call." Kelly smiled. "One of the reasons I wanted to go into a larger practice was to have the occasional weekend off. So once I leave the office, I'll be with the children until you and Ryan return, all married and happy."

"I appreciate you helping out like this," Ronni said. "I don't know what Ryan and I would have done without you. Tanner thinks he could handle Lia and Ryan's three, but we all know that's wishful thinking on his part."

Kelly waved aside her thanks. "I'm happy to do it." If anything, the weekend was going to be a lot of fun. She enjoyed being around children, and Tanner had promised to stay at the house, as well. She didn't want to admit to anyone, least of all herself, how her heart beat faster when he was around.

Ronni glanced at her suitcase. "I think that's everything. I just want to—"

A loud honk interrupted her. She froze. "Oh, no. It's the cab. I have to go. I'm not ready."

Alex stood up and patted her shoulder. "Don't panic. You're completely prepared. You have your wedding dress, your shoes and your makeup. Oh, and this." She fingered the lacy strap of Ronni's nightgown. "Nothing else matters."

"I know, but I think I want to scream anyway."

Kelly picked up her purse and Ronni's overnight

bag while Alex closed the larger suitcase. Ronni did a quick once-over of the room, then the three of them headed for the front door.

On the small porch, they hugged. "Have a wonderful wedding," Kelly said. "I have the phone numbers if anything happens, but remember that no news is good news. Just enjoy yourselves."

"Ditto what she said," Alex told Ronni. "Take deep breaths. You're going to be very happy with Ryan. Enjoy your time together."

"I will." Ronni waited while the cab driver loaded her luggage into the trunk, then she slid into the back seat.

Alex and Kelly stood watching her until the cab rounded a corner and Ronni was lost from sight.

Kelly sighed. "She's going to be a beautiful bride. I hope they remember to take pictures."

"Me, too. Speaking of beautiful, Wendy's baby is a charmer." Alex said, referring to her houseguest's new infant. "I thought I was happy with one child, but I have to tell you that having a newborn in the house is giving me second thoughts."

The two women started toward their cars parked at the curb.

"What about you," Alex asked. "Any second thoughts?"

"I'm not sure what you mean."

Alex paused by her car. "Something's different, Kelly, and I'm not sure what. Is it being around Tanner's daughter? I know you're spending a lot time at his house. Are you having thoughts about children of your own?"

Kelly drew in a deep breath. "My thoughts aren't that organized. I'm just...I don't know. Restless maybe.'' She pulled on her purse strap, securing it on her shoulder. ''Are you happy?'' she asked. ''With your life, I mean.''

''Yes,'' Alex answered slowly. ''I have a great life. I love my work. It's fulfilling in more ways than I'd thought possible. I have Tyler, who is the joy of my world.'' She smiled. ''To be honest, I have too many houseguests to ever worry about being lonely.''

''Is that enough?''

Alex looked surprised. ''Isn't it?''

''I don't know. I'm just rambling,'' Kelly admitted. ''But I can't help thinking about the fact that you spend all your free time with your four-year-old son and whomever is currently living in your guestroom. Right now it's Wendy and her newborn. We're talking about a teenage girl. I was just wondering if you kept your life so full because then there isn't room for a man.''

Alex pressed her lips together. ''Ouch. You don't believe in subtle, do you?''

''I'm sorry. I don't mean to be critical. I'm wondering aloud because I'm thinking these same thoughts about myself.''

''I know what you're saying,'' Alex told her, ''but I've done the man in my life bit, and it's not all it's cracked up to be. I like being on my own.''

''I do, too,'' Kelly said, but she couldn't help thinking that at times her life was a cold and empty place. Sometimes she wanted someone else to share things with. Someone she could depend on. Someone she could love who would love her back.

''Not to change the subject, but I have to get back

to work,'' Alex said, glancing at her watch. ''Are we still on for Sunday?''

''Absolutely. Griffin would kill me if we didn't meet you there.'' Griffin, Ryan's youngest, was best friends with Alex's son, Tyler. She and Alex had made arrangements to meet at a local pizza place for an afternoon of junk food and video games.

''I've got to run, too,'' Kelly said. ''See you on Sunday. About two, okay?''

''Perfect.'' Alex called out a quick good-bye, then got into her car.

Kelly followed more slowly. As she pulled out onto the street, she couldn't help thinking about what Alex had said about men. That they didn't live up to their hype. Kelly couldn't offer an opinion on the subject because she didn't have enough experience. Since high school, she'd gone out of her way to shut men out of her life. During college and medical school, she'd had lots of male friends, but no emotionally significant relationships. The question was why?

No one had really hurt her, not unless she counted her father's disappointment. Her high school boyfriend had dumped her when he'd found out she was pregnant, but while she'd been disappointed, she hadn't been devastated. She liked men. She thought many were attractive. There were times when she thought about making love with a certain man and she found herself feeling desire. So why turn her back on that part of her life?

She didn't have any answers, and then she found herself suddenly thinking about Tanner. She was attracted to the man—no question about that. She wanted to dismiss those feelings by saying he wasn't her type, except she didn't have a type. He was good-looking and while that was a nice plus, it wasn't the reason she found him appealing. Most of it was the man himself. How was she supposed to resist him when he was so devoted to his daughter? And easy to be with. And funny. And caring.

She sighed. So if Tanner Malone was so all-fired perfect, why wasn't he married? Or why wasn't there a line of women camped outside his house? Was it them, or was it him? Or was it something in his past…something she didn't know about?

So many secrets, Kelly thought. Even though the past was long over, it had a way of hanging around and influencing the present. She knew she was dealing with some issues of her own. Yesterday, when she and Tanner had been in Ronni's waiting room and he'd made a comment about her being so good with kids, she'd felt as if he'd ripped her heart out. It hadn't been his fault, of course. He had no way of knowing how much she'd wanted to be a pediatrician. It had been all she'd wanted when she was a young girl. Except it hadn't worked out that way.

Kelly turned the corner and headed toward her office. As she drove, she tried to figure out what had gone wrong. From the first day she'd entered medical school, every time she'd stepped into a hospital and had seen a young girl, she'd thought about her daughter…the child she'd given up for adoption. She wondered about the girl, about her parents. Eventually the guilt and pain grew to be too much. She decided that she didn't deserve to work with children, so she'd chosen something else. Something that allowed her to be around babies.

"It's not second best," she murmured to herself

as she pulled into her parking space. Except she wasn't sure she believed the words. Not that it mattered. It was too late to change now. Sometimes it was important to stand by one's choices, and she knew in her heart that this was one of those times.

"Can we make purple?" Tanner asked Saturday afternoon as he scanned the bowls of icing lined up on the kitchen table. "What is that, blue and red, right?" He looked to Kelly for confirmation.

She set down the sheet of cookies she'd just pulled out of the oven and laughed. "Tanner, you already have just about every color that ever existed. Yes, purple is a combination of red and blue, but you don't need to make it. Besides, I don't think there are any more bowls."

"I know where they are," six-year-old Lisbeth said helpfully. "Grandma keeps extra bowls in here." She dragged her chair over to a cupboard and climbed up, then pointed to the top shelf. "Up there."

"What a bright little girl you are," Tanner said as he reached above her head and snagged two more bowls. "Just in case the mixing process runs into trouble." He set the bowls on the table and dumped in a couple of spoonfuls of white icing. "Want to help me with this, Lisbeth?"

"Sure." The young girl returned to her uncle's side and grinned. "Don't add too much color. Remember what happened when you tried to make orange."

"I remember."

Kelly glanced at the sink, which was filled with bowls glowing with rejected colors. It was going to take a week to get everything cleaned up. She smiled. Not that she wanted to be anywhere but here. She was having the best time.

"Aunt Kelly?" Drew, Ryan's oldest, moved up next to her.

"Yes, Drew. Did you want to ice cookies?" She pointed to the dozens already cooling on the rack. Somehow tripling the recipe for sugar cookies had produced more cookies than she'd expected. They were going to have to freeze a bunch.

"You know they sell cookies at the store," he said, his voice low as if he didn't want his brother and sister to hear. "That would have been easier for you and Uncle Tanner than making them."

Drew was only nine, but he was plenty responsible. His big blue eyes were filled with concern. "I don't want to be rude, but you're not really used to kids and the three of us are a real handful."

Kelly set the cookie sheet on the counter, then dropped to her knees and pulled Drew close. "You know what? I think I can handle it. But you're a sweetie for being concerned."

"Okay. If you're sure." He didn't look the least bit convinced. "I guess this is practice for when you have your own children."

"I hadn't thought of it that way, but you're right."

He glanced over his shoulder, then leaned close and whispered in her ear. "Uncle Tanner is really good with Lia. I didn't think he'd like having a baby, but he does."

Kelly touched his face. "You're not really nine, are you? You're actually a thirty year old disguised as a nine year old."

Drew shook his head. "I'm nine."

"I don't know."

"He's just responsible, like Ryan was," Tanner said from his seat at the table. "It comes from being the oldest."

"So if I'm the oldest, like my dad, were you the youngest?"

"Yup."

Drew's gaze narrowed. "So you were like Griffin?"

Together the three of them looked at Ryan's youngest son, who was all of four. He sat pulled up close to the table, with six cookies spread out in front of him. His intense expression never wavered as he focused on getting just the exact amount of icing on each of his cookies. Of course there was also icing on the front of his shirt, coating his hands and all over his face. Not to mention several globs in his hair.

Kelly covered her mouth to hold in a giggle. Tanner looked a little indignant. "I wasn't exactly like him," he said.

"I'd hope not," Kelly said. She turned to Drew. "I have to tell you that your uncle is a little too big and grown up for me to imagine him like Griffin."

"Maybe," Drew agreed, glancing from his brother to his uncle.

"But I still like to ice cookies," Tanner said, holding out a bowl for them to inspect.

Kelly pursed her lips. "All right. I've got to hand it to you. That's a great shade of purple."

He'd created a dark, vibrant color that would look perfect on the cookies, but probably would be difficult to get out of clothes. She held back a sigh. If the kids ended up with stains on their shirts, Ronni and Ryan weren't going to be so thrilled by her offer to baby-sit.

A faint snuffling sound caught her attention. She glanced up and saw that Tanner had heard the noise, too. He was already pushing back his chair. "I'll go check on Lia," he said as he walked past the baby monitor.

Kelly surveyed the mess that used to be a very nice kitchen. Somehow she and Tanner would get it all cleaned up. The clothes would come clean and regardless of the hours spent to make things right again, it would be worth it. She couldn't remember the last time she'd had this much fun.

"My dad says that Lia is good for Uncle Tanner," Drew said as he settled back in his chair and reached for a cookie. He studied the bowls, then picked up the yellow one and reached for a popsicle stick which he used to smooth on the rapidly hardening icing. "Dad says it will settle him down."

Drew looked up at her and frowned. "Not that Uncle Tanner is, you know, wild."

"Of course not," she agreed, wondering where this conversation was heading. She had a feeling that Drew had been listening to talk that might not have been meant for his nine-year-old ears, as it was unlikely that Ryan would discuss his brother with his young son.

"He's very nice and caring. He's a great uncle." Drew made a circle on the round cookie, then started making eyes and a big smile. "It's just that Lia gives him a family of his own. Dad says he'll be getting married soon. Do *you* think Uncle Tanner is a good dad?"

He asked his question with the studied casualness of someone pretending not to care about the answer, when in fact he was deeply interested. Suddenly all the odd statements and comments made sense. She stood facing a nine-year-old matchmaker. And perhaps his matchmaking father as well. For all she knew, Ronni was in on it.

Kelly waited for a couple of seconds, then decided that she wasn't angry. Ryan and Drew and everyone else were just trying to make sure that Tanner was happy. If they thought Kelly was a likely candidate, of course they would encourage any relationship. Too bad she and Tanner were just friends. Everyone was destined to be disappointed when they found out.

Tanner walked back into the kitchen. He held Lia in his arms. She stared at all the activity and her big eyes got bigger. Pink fists flailed about and her rosebud mouth puckered into a pretty decent facsimile of a smile.

"How's the cookie detail coming?" he asked.

Kelly glanced at the mess on the table. Less than half the cookies were iced, but she sensed that the kids were getting tired of helping. "I think they're pretty close to done. I thought I'd finish up frosting while they watch a movie."

Lisbeth glanced up, a smudge of blue icing on her cheek. "What are we going to watch?"

Drew and Griffin offered opinions at the same time. Lisbeth protested. The sound volume in the room increased. Kelly met Tanner's gaze and smiled. Yes, it was chaos, but she had to admit it was also everything she'd ever wanted. All her life, she'd longed for a big family. While her father had loved her deeply, and had always been there for her, his ministry had kept him busy. Besides, he wasn't another kid she could play with.

She'd started baby-sitting as soon as she was old enough. She'd adored infants, toddlers, little kids, even teenagers. Every stage had its ups and downs and she'd wanted to experience them all. Somewhere along the way, her dream had gotten lost. Was there a way to get it back or was it too late?

"Actually," Tanner said loudly into the din, "Lia was telling me that she would like to watch *A Bug's Life,* and as she's the guest here, I think it's her choice."

All three children stared at him. "Lia can't talk," Lisbeth said.

"Not very well," he admitted, "but I know what she's thinking."

"Is that so?" Kelly asked.

"Sure." Tanner's blue eyes danced with laughter. "Besides, the princess in the movie is pretty cute."

"I thought this was Lia's choice."

"It is, but I happen to agree with her."

"Uncle Tanner, you don't get to pick," Lisbeth insisted. "You're not a kid."

Drew shook his head. "You'd better let him. Otherwise, he'll be cranky all night."

"I'm not cranky," Tanner said, even as he headed for the family room. "Why would you say I'm cranky? We can arm wrestle to see who picks. Griffin, want to arm wrestle with Uncle Tanner?"

Kelly watched the three children trail after their uncle. She couldn't help smiling. Life around Tanner was certainly interesting. When he didn't need her anymore and she returned to her old ways, things were going to seem very quiet. But for now, she was living in the center of chaos and it felt wonderful.

"How do you know they live happily ever after?" Lisbeth asked with a yawn as she burrowed her head deeper into her pillow.

"Because it's a fairy tale and that's always how they end. It's the point."

"Will I live happily ever after?"

"Of course," Kelly said, kissing her cheek. "We always have challenges to keep us growing as people, but on the whole life is generally happy."

Lisbeth rolled onto her side. She didn't take up much room in the single bed, but she was surrounded by an army of stuffed animals. They crowded her feet and legs, leaned on her pillow and pressed up against her back.

"Go to sleep," Kelly said as she stood.

Tanner pushed off from the wall where he'd been leaning and approached his niece. "Night, Lisbeth. You have sweet dreams."

"I will." She held out her arms to hug him.

He'd always thought she was so small, but she wasn't when compared with Lia. Funny, but he couldn't picture his own daughter ever being so big. Or worse, talking. Kelly had handled Lisbeth's question about living happily ever after with an ease that he couldn't imagine. If it had been him, he would have hemmed and hawed before coming up with some philosophical reply that only would have confused her. Parenting was harder than it looked.

"I love you, Uncle Tanner," she murmured.

He kissed her forehead. "I love you, too, kiddo. Now go to sleep."

But instead of resting her head back on the pillow, she grinned slyly. "I think you should kiss Kelly good-night."

Tanner didn't dare turn around to glance at Kelly. He wasn't sure he wanted to know what she was thinking. "Do you now?"

"Uh huh. A nice, big kiss, like the way Daddy kisses Ronni when he thinks we're not watching."

"I'll have to tell your father that you *are* watching. What do you think of that, you minx?"

She giggled.

He kissed her forehead again. "Go to sleep."

"What about Kelly?"

He stood up and clicked off the bedside lamp. "That's none of your business. We'll see you in the morning."

"Okay. Night."

He followed Kelly out of her room and into the hallway. Griffin was already asleep and Drew was tucked in his bed, reading. Tanner tried not to notice the quiet of the house, or the dim lighting in the hall. Had it looked this intimate before? He couldn't remember.

"Sorry about that," he said quietly as he shut the door behind him. "I can't figure out why the kids are behaving like this."

"They're matchmaking," Kelly said lightly. "What I can't figure is who put them up to it."

"The list of suspects is long. I'd guess everyone from Ryan to Ronni. Maybe even the kids' grandmother." He shrugged. "I hope it doesn't make you uncomfortable."

"Not at all. I think it's pretty funny. Are you okay with it?"

Maybe it was the silence of the night, he thought as he resisted the need to step closer to her. Maybe it was the fact that he could inhale the sweet scent of her body. Or maybe it was just plain stupidity on his part. Regardless, he found himself wanting to pull her hard against him and kiss her, just like Lisbeth had requested. He wanted to kiss her the way a man kissed a woman he's attracted to.

Instead he swallowed. "Yeah, I'm fine. You're right. The situation is pretty funny." He cleared his throat. "So, ah, do you want to watch some television?"

"Sure. It's a little early to go to bed."

"Great."

But neither of them moved. He motioned toward the stairs. "The family room is down there."

"I know."

Damn. Had it gotten hot in here, or was it just him? He tugged at the collar of his shirt. "Kelly, I..."

"Yes?"

Had her eyes always been dark, bottomless pools? And was it his imagination or did her body seem to be swaying toward him? Lord help him, he wanted her.

"Either we go downstairs right now or I'm going to have to kiss you," he told her.

"Are those my two choices?"

"Yeah."

She smiled. "Hmm, I'm going to have to think about them for a while."

"Are you?"

She nodded.

He took a step closer, then placed one hand on her waist. "Here. Let me help you decide." Then he lowered his mouth to hers.

Chapter Eleven

They had only kissed once before, yet Kelly had a sense of coming home as she stepped into Tanner's embrace. His arms were as strong as she remembered, his chest as broad, his taste as sweet. When his lips pressed against hers, it was easy to surrender to the passion flaring between them, to simply rest her belly against his arousal and it was the most natural thing in the world to touch her tongue to his.

They both wore casual clothes and athletic shoes, so he was only a couple of inches taller than her. She raised her arms until they rested on his broad shoulders, then leaned against him. His big hands stretched across her back, holding her...perhaps in place...perhaps just touching. Either was fine with her. She had no plans to disappear. Being close to Tanner, feeling his strength, his heat and his desire, was the best part of her day. She couldn't imagine anyone else feeling so right in her embrace.

He tilted his head slightly, then plunged his tongue into her mouth. She welcomed him, touching him, circling around, teasing him. He let her play her game, then returned the sensual torture, exploring her mouth, stroking against her in a way designed to make her whimper.

Their closeness ignited a fire inside of her. The flames didn't just flicker gently with a sensual warmth. Instead she found herself consumed by a conflagration that left her breathless and weak. The muscles of her legs trembled. Her breasts swelled and ached, and between her thighs she felt the swelling and dampness that foretold her body's readiness for this man's very male invasion.

Tanner broke the kiss, but before she could protest, he licked her lower lip, then nibbled at the corner of her mouth. She found it difficult to continue to hold her head upright. When he kissed a damp trail down to her neck, it was easy to tilt her head to the side and allow him to have his way with her.

Light, teasing, tickling kisses made her shiver. He bit her ear lobe, then soothed the erotic hurt with his tongue. He breathed her name against the hollow of her throat, he kissed his way to the other side of her neck and back up to her mouth. Every action stirred her more deeply and left her wanting in a way she'd never wanted a man before in her life.

His hardness pressed against her belly. She flexed her hips and rubbed up and down wanting *him* to want with the same fierceness. He groaned low in his throat.

"You're killing me," he murmured against her mouth.

"Me, too."

"Don't stop."

He licked at the seam of her lips, but when they parted, he didn't invade. Instead he touched the tip of her tongue with his and retreated. When she didn't respond, he repeated the action. Kelly finally realized that he wanted her to follow, to play a very grown-up version of tag.

The next time he tagged her as "it" she went after him, delving into his mouth, exploring him as he had explored her. She learned the tastes and textures of him, felt the smoothness of his teeth, the faint roughness of his tongue. Unexpectedly his lips clamped around her and he sucked gently.

The incredible sensation sent lightning flaring through her woman's place and down her legs. She shuddered and pressed harder against him, needing him, desperate for more contact.

He pulled back slightly and rained kisses on her face.

"No," she gasped, reaching up to hold him in place, then kissing him again, practically attacking him. He chuckled, then plunged into her mouth, stroking her, exciting her, making her want to rip her clothes off and beg him to take her right there.

Thank goodness he could read her mind. His hands settled on her waist, then moved up under the loose sweatshirt she'd pulled on that morning. Strong, warm fingers traced her ribs, making her shiver, before he cupped her breasts against his palms.

Kelly considered herself fairly average on top.

Not small, but not huge either. Tanner held her breasts in a way that made her think they'd been designed specifically with his hands in mind. Or maybe it was the other way around. Regardless, as he gently explored her curves, lightly rubbing his palms against her puckered nipples, she felt herself grow hotter.

One of his hands moved behind her for a second. She felt a faint tug, then her bra loosened. Tanner pulled up her sweatshirt, lowered his head and took her nipple in his mouth.

The feel of his damp lips and tongue nearly made her scream. She had to hold onto him to keep from collapsing. Heat and need built inside of her until she thought she couldn't stand it. Muscles quivered. If she hadn't known better she would have thought that she might climax right then...just because he was touching her breasts. But that wasn't possible. They were standing in a hallway, both fully dressed. It was crazy to think that—

Tanner swore, then stood up. He clutched her shoulders and pressed his forehead to hers. "I'm about to lose it and we know this is neither the time nor the place. Right?"

"Right."

They both sounded hoarse, their voices thick with passion.

"You're amazing," he told her. "I want you so much."

"And I want you."

But he was right. There were four children in the house. They were supposed to be baby-sitting. Regardless of how turned on she felt now, Kelly knew that she wouldn't be comfortable if they took things any further. She was glad they'd stopped. Really. Except every part of her ached for Tanner. How had things gotten so hot so fast? The man could turn her on with a look.

She reached behind her and refastened her bra, then straightened her sweatshirt. "Thanks," she whispered.

"Oh, it was my pleasure and I mean that." Tanner studied her.

"What?" she asked. "Why are you staring?"

"I'm trying to learn your secrets."

She frowned. As far as she knew, she didn't have many. "What secrets?"

"I want to know why you aren't married." He reached up and touched her face. "Don't even think about giving me the 'I've been so busy' line. We both know it's more than that."

What was she supposed to say? Kelly didn't have an answer. She opened her mouth, then closed it and shrugged.

"Not good enough, Dr. Hall. You're an amazing woman. Bright, beautiful, sexy as hell. If you'd kept rubbing against me like that I would have embarrassed us both."

She smiled. "I wouldn't have been embarrassed."

"It would have done me in." He paused.

She knew he was waiting for an answer. "I'm not hiding anything, Tanner. I'm as confused as you are. I think it's a combination of things. I've been thinking about this a lot lately and I think it's my past, and fear, and maybe circumstances. I'm not sure. What's your excuse?"

She'd expected him to make some flippant response. Instead he said, "I'm a screwup. Look at what happened when I went to college."

She took his hand and led him to the top of the stairs where they both sat. Their shoulders brushed against each other. "I don't believe that," she said. "It took you a little while to get it all together. So what? Some people aren't ready for college at eighteen. They need to figure a few things out first."

"Maybe. I guess I'm something of a late bloomer. It takes me a while to get it together."

"Now you have Lia."

"Yeah. A child."

But no wife.

Neither of them spoke the phrase, but Kelly suspected they were both thinking the same thing. Was he ready now? If so, where did that leave her? Did she care? Did she want to care?

"I think we're both in a transition stage in our lives," she said carefully. "That's not a healthy time to get involved in anything…" She paused. "You know, personal."

He turned toward her. "Is that your professional opinion?"

"I'm not a psychiatrist. But it is my opinion, professional or otherwise."

"I see." He tucked a loose strand of her hair behind her ear. "And if I were to kiss you right now?"

Instantly her body went up in flames. It took every ounce of strength she had to keep from swaying toward him. "I'm not sure I could resist."

He smiled. "Thanks for telling me that." He leaned close and brushed a kiss across her mouth. "Go to bed, Dr. Kelly Hall. Go right now or I won't be responsible for my actions."

She hesitated. What did she want? Was it Tanner? Or did she want the safety of her boring, impersonal life? Then she glanced around at the unfamiliar house and realized that regardless of what she wanted, she couldn't forget where they were.

"Good night," she said regretfully as she rose to her feet.

He didn't say anything. He just watched her walk toward the guest room. She had a feeling it was going to be a long time before either of them slept.

The cacophony of the video games blended perfectly with the sound of shrieking, screaming children. Kelly glanced around at the madness that was Pizza Pete's and was incredibly grateful she wasn't prone to headaches. She looked at the child in her arms, but Lia slept on, apparently unaware of the frenzy around her.

"The woman on the phone turned out to be one of Wendy's aunts," Alex was saying, her voice raised to be heard over the din. As she spoke to Kelly, she kept her gaze fixed on her son, Tyler, and Griffin, who were intensely concentrating on a game that involved hitting a fake gopher with a sponge bat. The gopher popped out of different holes in the ground and so far had eluded even a single bop to his plastic head.

"I didn't know Wendy had any family other than her mother," Kelly said. Wendy, the pregnant teenager who had moved in with Alex until her baby was born, had told Kelly that she was pretty much alone in the world.

"I guess it didn't occur to Wendy that anyone would help her. After all, her own mother threw her out when she found out the girl was pregnant.'' Alex shook her head. Her short brown hair flew around her face before falling back into its perfect wedge. ''I don't understand parents like that. But it's turned out well. The aunt wants to give Wendy and her baby a home and good start. Apparently this aunt is a teacher and her semester will be up in a couple of weeks. Wendy's going to stay with me until then.''

Kelly studied her friend. ''You don't look happy about her leaving.''

''I'm not,'' Alex admitted. ''She's a terrific young woman and I'll confess to adoring her baby. But this is going to be good for her. She's going to sign up for community college and go after her degree.''

''Just think, you'll have a spare bedroom again,'' Kelly teased. ''How long until it fills up again?''

Alex laughed. ''I'd like to have a week of peace, but I have no expectations.''

''Uh oh. I know that look. Who's next?''

''No one.'' Alex hesitated, then moved her plastic soda glass in a circle on the picnic table. ''Okay, there's this kid. Brett. He's sixteen and really doing well since his surgery, but he needs to start rehabilitation. His insurance doesn't cover living expenses while he's in rehab and he lives too far away to commute. I haven't decided yet, but I'm thinking of offering him a room with me. Just while he recovers.''

''You're amazing,'' Kelly said. For as long as she'd known Alex, the other woman had been giving room and board to a parade of strangers in need.

''We've had this conversation before.'' She paused as Tyler came running up.

"We got 'em!" he crowed. "Did ya see, Mom? Griffin got him twice and I got him once."

"Good for you. Want to play again?"

Tyler nodded furiously. Alex handed them each another quarter and the two boys took off. Kelly looked around for Tanner, Drew and Lisbeth, then spotted them entering the laser tag arena.

"I don't know how you did it," Kelly said, her gaze moving to Tyler. "I thought residency was hard enough on its own, but you had a child."

Alex shifted on the hard seat. "I'll admit to being tired a lot of the time. Having a baby terrified me, mostly because I didn't know anything about them. But we're muddling through together."

"It's more than muddling. You're both thriving."

"Maybe," Alex said. "It helped that I was so far along in my studies. I think if I'd been in medical school I wouldn't have made it. But I was well into my residency when he was born."

Kelly thought of her own past. She'd been seventeen when she'd gotten pregnant. She hadn't even been to college, let alone medical school.

"Did you always want to be an orthopedist?" Kelly asked.

"Absolutely." Alex grinned. "When I was all of twelve my dad helped me with a bird I'd found. Its wing was broken. I still remember how stunned I was that the wing actually healed and the bird was able to fly away. From that moment on I knew I wanted to do the same thing for people."

"There aren't a lot of women in that field," Kelly said.

"Tell me about it. There have been problems, but I've survived. What about you? Did you change your specialty? I know most students have trouble deciding.''

Kelly drew in a deep breath. ''I'd wanted to be a pediatrician but that didn't work out.''

''Too bad.'' Alex nodded at the sleeping infant. ''You're good with them, but then you're good at what you do now. Think of the mothers and babies you've saved. Besides, we women have to stick together.''

Kelly made herself smile, even though she could feel the familiar sadness filling her. So many questions. Had she made the right choice with her daughter and had she made the right choice with her career? Not that it mattered. It was too late to change either decision.

''Enough being serious,'' Alex said as she slapped her palms on the table. ''Come on. We'll challenge the guys to a race. I know it's silly but I love those car video games. Where else can people crash into walls and walk away without even a bruise?''

Kelly followed her toward the collection of free-standing video games. Tanner, Lisbeth and Drew appeared to be talking excitedly about their game of laser tag.

''You hit me fifteen times,'' Lisbeth complained as she studied her score sheet.

Tanner looked sheepish. ''You're an easy target, kid. What can I say. I hit Drew a bunch, too.''

''Yeah, but I didn't hit either of you once,'' Lisbeth said.

''You didn't hit anyone,'' Drew pointed out. ''But don't worry. You'll do better next time.''

"He's right," Tanner said, pulling the little girl close. "Besides, you're prettier than both of us."

"And smarter," she insisted.

Tanner laughed. "Maybe."

As Kelly watched him, she couldn't help remembering her own past. Her father had been wonderful with her. He'd expected a high standard of behavior, but no matter what, she'd always felt he loved her. As she cradled Lia close, she knew that Tanner was going to be the same kind of father. Gentle, kind, yet always teaching and showing by example.

"How are you holding up?" Tanner asked.

"Fine." She motioned to Lia. "She's wet, so I thought I'd go change her. I'd make you do it, but I doubt there's a changing station in the men's restroom."

"Saved by inequality," Tanner teased. "Thanks for taking care of her while I was with the other kids."

"It's hardly difficult. I adore her."

"Me, too."

Their gazes locked and she knew they were both thinking about what had happened last night. And what had *not* happened. The kiss had come close to leading to something else. Something neither of them was ready for. But had it become inevitable? A shiver rippled through her.

She turned and made her way toward the restrooms at the rear of the building. As she moved through the crowd, she heard a man yelling at his daughter. Kelly held Lia close, grateful this little girl wasn't going to have to deal with a difficult parent. She would always be loved, as Kelly had been loved...right up until she got pregnant. That was the one thing her father couldn't forgive. Was that why she couldn't forgive herself?

She reached the restroom. The door pushed open and three teenage girls stepped out. They were talking and laughing and didn't even notice her. But she studied them, wondering if any of the three looked like her daughter. Annie Jane was nearly fourteen. Practically a young woman.

Then, as she'd done a thousand times in the past, she pushed away the aching inside of her and focused on the task at hand. She'd lost the right to worry about her daughter the day she'd made the decision to give her away.

Several open boxes of pizza covered the wooden picnic tables. "But I wanted soda," Drew said.

"Thanks for the info, but we agreed on milk," Kelly told him mildly.

"You agreed. I wanted soda."

Kelly stared at the nine year old. "Drew, if you're going to be difficult, I want to take this discussion outside."

Tanner waited, breath held, then his nephew nodded once. "Sorry, Kelly. Milk is fine."

"Good." She set a glass in front of him.

The mini drama was like a dozen others that had been played out today. Pizza Pete's was a lot of fun, but it also stressed the kids and the adults. Still, as Tanner glanced around the crowded table, he knew there wasn't anywhere else he would rather be. He had his daughter in his arms, his family nearby, good company, halfway decent food. Life didn't get much better than this.

"Do you like my hair, Uncle Tanner?" Lisbeth

asked. She spun her head back and forth to show off the ribbons she'd won earlier. Kelly had braided them into her hair.

"You look lovely," he said. "I think you're the prettiest little girl here."

Lisbeth giggled and blushed. Then Griffin knocked over his milk.

Kelly started to stand up but Tanner motioned her to stay seated. "My turn," he said. He shifted Lia to his left arm, then climbed out from the picnic table and headed for the counter. There he ordered another milk and grabbed a fistful of napkins.

"Isn't she a beauty," a woman said.

Tanner saw a petite blonde smiling at Lia. She turned her attention to Tanner. "Yours?"

"Yup."

He took the milk and pocketed his change. Unfortunately the woman didn't seem inclined to let him slip by. She stood firmly in his way.

"Does she look like your wife?" the woman asked.

"I'm not married."

"Oh."

There was a wealth of meaning in that single word. At one time in his life, Tanner might have been willing to take the woman up on her offer. After all she was around his age, pretty enough, and willing. For a while, that had been all he'd needed. But not anymore.

The woman sighed. "So you're a single dad. You're doing a great job." She pointed to a collection of boys by a martial arts video game. "Two of those are mine. It's their dad's weekend, but the jerk flakes out on a regular basis."

"That's too bad." Tanner inched past her. "If you'll excuse me, I have to get back to my family."

He pointed toward the picnic table and she glanced in that direction. Her welcoming expression faded. "Oh. Is one of them yours?"

He assumed she was speaking about Alex and Kelly, not all the children. "Yes."

"I see. Fine." She spun on her heel and left.

Tanner made his way to the table and took his seat. He dropped the extra napkins onto the puddle of milk and handed Griffin a new carton.

As Griffin took it, he wrinkled his nose. "Sorry, Uncle Tanner. I'm more careful now."

"I'm sure you will be."

"I knew I was right," Kelly said as he settled next to her. "But I never thought to have it proven to me."

"What?" he asked, even though he knew exactly what she was talking about.

She pointed to the sleeping baby in his arms. "Lia *is* a chick magnet."

He frowned. "Do you really think I care about that?"

"I'm not sure. Now that you have a child, the next most obvious step is to get involved with a woman. A single mother is a good match." She looked across the table toward her friend. "Alex is a single mother."

Tanner didn't understand. Was Kelly suggesting that he get involved with Alex? How could he? She was certainly very nice and he liked her a lot, but last night Kelly had been the one he'd been holding and the one he'd wanted to make love with.

"I heard that," Alex said, grinning. "And while

Tanner might be in the market for a mate, I don't think I'm who he has in mind.''

He glanced at the woman sitting across from him. Alex gave him a knowing look. So she knew he had a thing for Kelly. At one time the information might have bothered him, but not anymore.

''Speaking of which,'' Kelly said brightly, ''I'm going to be giving Tanner a baby shower. Actually the shower is for Lia, but you know what I mean.''

''What a great idea,'' Alex told her, then winked at Tanner.

He had to smile back. As change of subjects went, it wasn't very subtle on Kelly's part. So she was a little flustered, was she? Good. Let her stay that way.

Kelly and Alex continued to talk about the shower. Drew asked to be excused to go play with his friends. Griffin and Tyler ate with enough energy to smear pizza sauce past their elbows and ears, while Lisbeth hummed loudly to herself. It was loud and messy and for the first time in his life, Tanner felt as if he'd found a place to belong.

Chapter Twelve

Late Sunday night Tanner paced through his house. Ronni and Ryan had arrived home a few hours before, looking in love and blissfully happy. He and Kelly had left together, but they'd parted ways. Now he wished he'd taken her up on her offer to come over to help him with Lia. Not that he needed help with his daughter—she was currently sleeping peacefully in her crib—but because he wanted to spend time with Kelly.

He couldn't stop thinking about her. About how she'd looked all weekend with the kids. She'd been fun, funny, patient and infinitely beautiful…even with icing smudged on her cheek. He also couldn't stop thinking about that incredible kiss they'd shared. It had been passionate and intense and dangerous. Dangerous because he knew better than to get involved.

He didn't want or need the complication. He didn't want to risk caring and losing again. At one time he'd lost everything important in his life. His parents, his brother when they were put into different foster homes, and his scholarship, although that was more his own fault than anyone else's. But the point was that he didn't have a lot of good luck when it came to things lasting. A long time ago he'd learned that if he didn't care, he couldn't get hurt.

Unfortunately...or maybe fortunately...he found himself on the verge of getting involved. With Kelly.

The smart thing would be to walk way, he told himself. He didn't need her or the complications a relationship would bring. They were both busy people moving in different directions. They didn't want the same things. So it was better to stay friends, nothing more. He would start pulling back right away.

But first he was going to call her.

Telling himself he was ten kinds of fool, Tanner walked down the stairs and picked up the kitchen phone. He dialed Kelly's number from memory, then listened to it ring.

"Hello?"

"Hi. It's Tanner." He paused. Now what? "I don't have an excuse for calling," he said. "I just want to see you. Naked." That last bit had dropped out of his mouth without warning, but it was too late to call it back. Besides, it was the truth.

He heard her breath catch, then a long silence. "Talk about coming right to the point," she murmured, sounding slightly stunned.

Disappointment overwhelmed him. He could

practically see her frantically trying to come up with a way to let him down gently. Keep it light, he told himself. Don't let 'em see you sweat. "Hey, don't worry about it," he told her. "You can say no and we'll still be friends."

"Thanks for telling me that. I'm just not sure I want to, um, say no." She cleared her throat. "The thing is, I'm not the trashy lingerie type."

Desire, need, elation, all of it slammed into his gut. Was she really saying yes? "I can honestly say that I wouldn't care if you wore a space suit. I'm a lot more concerned with what's underneath."

"Yes, well, okay. Tanner?"

He gripped the phone more tightly. "Yeah?"

"What are we doing?"

"Hell if I know. And before you scold me, Lia's upstairs. She didn't hear me swear."

She laughed softly, then sighed. "You know this is crazy. I mean it's a bad time for us, emotionally. You're dealing with Lia and all the changes she represents. I'm just barely beginning to understand that there are some issues from my past that I'm going to have to come to terms with."

"I know that."

"What I'm saying is that we're going to have be mature about this. I won't deny that I want you, but I'm not sure becoming lovers is wise. We're going to have to remember that this is about friends becoming intimate and nothing more. I don't want either of us to misrepresent or misunderstand the situation."

"Kelly?"

"Yes?"

"Are you going to talk all night or do you plan to get your perky butt over here?"

There was a moment of silence. "Do you have condoms or do you want me to bring them?"

He sucked in his breath. Talk about getting right to the point times two. "I can scrounge up a few."

"A few?"

"Hey, it's been a long time."

"I'd say no more than ten months."

"Ouch. Okay, ten months. But there hasn't been anyone since Lucy."

"It's been a while for me, too." She swallowed. "I'll be right over."

"I'll be waiting."

"Are you going to answer the door naked?"

He laughed. "Do you want me to?"

"I don't think so. I'm nervous already. That would probably send me screaming into the night."

"Then I'll keep my clothes on. But not for long."

"I can't wait." She hung up the phone.

Kelly stood on the front porch of Tanner's house and tried not to hyperventilate. She couldn't believe she was going to do this...or that *they* were going to be doing this. What had she been thinking? Or maybe she hadn't been thinking. How could she be expected to maintain rational thought when someone like Tanner Malone called her on the phone and told her he wanted to see her naked?

She sucked in a deep breath. This was dangerous territory, she knew that. It had been years since she'd been involved with anyone, and she knew with certainty that she'd spent her entire adult life avoiding anything like a real relationship. She wanted to tell herself that this was just about sex...nothing more. Except she didn't believe it.

Which meant, if she was smart, she would turn on her heel and head right back to her car. Only a brainless woman eager for trouble or heartache would push that doorbell.

She knocked on the door. *Oh God, oh God, oh God I can't do this,* she told herself and took a single step back. Just then Tanner opened the door.

He stood in front of her, backlit by the lamp in the living room. He was big and strong and about the sexiest man she'd ever seen. It didn't matter that he was casually dressed in jeans and sweatshirt. The soft, baggy shirt merely emphasized the breadth of his shoulders, while his jeans had worn white in interesting places.

"Kelly?"

"Huh?" She blinked.

"Hi," he said, and motioned for her to enter the house.

She did, stumbling over the threshold and then having to take three quick steps to regain her balance. She groaned under her breath. This was going to be worse than she'd thought.

"Look, Tanner," she began, backing away from him. "It's not that I'm having second thoughts, it's just that I'm nervous. I don't do this sort of thing every day."

"Really?" He sounded surprised as he closed the door, locked it, then flipped off the lamp.

She glanced around and realized that something flickered in the empty room. Then she saw the logs burning brightly in the over-sized fireplace. In front of the stone hearth was a thick blanket, a couple of pillows, and an ice bucket with wine or champagne.

Her throat tightened. "You do seduction right, don't you?" she said, then winced when her voice quivered a little. "It's okay. Really. I'm fine with this. But maybe we could, you know, talk some before getting right down to doing it."

Tanner chuckled. "It? What exactly is 'it'?"

"It's, well, it. Sex."

"Sex? Is that what you're here for?" He took a step toward her. "I'm not interested in sex."

She glanced nervously from the blanket to fire and back to him. "We're going to play cards instead?"

"No. We're going to make love. I've done both and to be honest, I'm not much interested in sex anymore. That was something I did when I was young and foolish. Now I prefer to make love with someone I care about." He took another step toward her. "Someone I respect." Another step. He was getting very, very close. "Someone I find incredibly sexy."

She made a little squeaking sound. "Me?"

"Yes, you."

In the dim light of the flickering fire his eyes were more black than blue. Despite the fact that he was only a couple of inches taller, he seemed to loom above her like a giant. She felt small and fragile and incredibly aroused. Unfortunately, she was more nervous than anything else, and it was all she could do to stand her ground. It would be so easy to turn and run.

"But we can talk first, if that would help you

relax," he said, moving forward again. He stopped directly in front of her.

He was close enough that she could inhale the familiar scent of his body and feel his heat. He reached toward her and slipped her large tote off her shoulder. Not sure if she was spending the night, Kelly had thrown a couple of things into a bag so she wouldn't be caught without a toothbrush in the morning.

"So how long do you want me to stay?" she asked as he set her tote on the floor. "I mean are you a do it and leave kind of guy, or do you like to cuddle after?"

He cupped her face. "Is there somewhere you have to be in the morning?"

"Yes. Work. We both have to be there."

"Good point. Okay, stay as long as you're comfortable. I'd like you to spend the night, but you don't have to."

She nodded. "I think I'll play it by ear."

"Good idea. Speaking of which…"

He leaned in close and kissed the sensitive skin just behind her ear. Then he drew the lobe into his mouth and sucked. She stiffened as fire shot through her and her breath caught in her already tight throat. How was she supposed to think when he was doing that?

"I thought we were going to talk," she whispered. "To help me relax."

"You can talk," he told her. "I'll listen."

But he was already trailing kisses down her throat. Her sweater had a modest V-neck. Tanner nibbled his way to the bottom of the V, then licked the skin not quite exposed by the soft knit. Her thighs shook, then began to smolder as her blood heated to near boiling. Already her breasts were uncomfortably swollen.

"You're not talking," he said as his hands settled on her waist. He tugged at the hem of her sweater and before she could figure out what he was doing, he'd pulled it over her head.

So much for conversation. But oddly enough, Kelly found she didn't mind. She knew that the only way to get over her case of nerves was to do the one thing she was afraid of. Which meant making love with Tanner.

She noticed he was staring at her bra. "You lied," he said.

Now it was her turn to feel in control. "I said I didn't have trashy lingerie. This isn't trashy."

He fingered the strap of the peach silk and lace bra. "It's beautiful. Not as beautiful as what it covers, but still very nice."

She raised her arms until they rested on his shoulders, then she pressed herself against him. "You're not the only one who gets lingerie catalogues in the mail. The difference is I order from them. Now do you want to talk all night, or do you want to make love?"

Instead of answering in words, he wrapped his arms around her, hauled her hard against him and plundered her mouth.

She was ready for his assault and more than met him half way. As his lips pressed against hers, she parted, welcoming his tongue with eager strokes and thrusts. His taste was sweet and intoxicating. She adored how she could remember his flavor. She knew that if she licked his arm or his belly that he would taste similar there as well. Variations on a theme—the essences of this wonderful man.

She clutched his head, burying her fingers into his thick hair. With her free hand she caressed his shoulders. His muscles bunched under her touch, coiling and uncoiling in a demonstration of his strength. His hands moved up and down her bare back. He was warm and smooth. She shivered when one hand reached down to stroke her fanny. He slipped it down the back of her thigh, then pulled gently, urging her to lift her leg up to his hip.

The position brought her hot, ready center into contact with his rock-hard thigh. Involuntarily her hips flexed forward as she sought some release from the building tension. At the same time his arousal pressed into her. Without thinking, she slipped a hand between them and cupped him.

Instantly Tanner stiffened, sucked in a breath and exhaled her name. "You can't do that," he told her, releasing her leg and taking a step back. "Jeez, Kelly, I want to make this good for you, but it's been a hell of a long time for me and I really want you." His tense expression turned rueful. "Just think of me as a teenager facing his first time. The slightest touch will make me finish in about a tenth of a second."

"Really?" His confession surprised her. She would have thought that he'd been with enough women that one more wasn't all that special. "How much of this is time and how much of it is me?"

As soon as she asked the question, she wanted to call it back. She accepted the fact that she was pretty okay-looking. Not gorgeous, but not hideous, either. However, she was not in Tanner's league, looks-wise. If Lucy had been average for him, then Kelly didn't have a prayer.

"It's about ninety-ten," he said.

"Oh." Ninety percent time. Well, at least she had her ten percent. That was something. She tried to ignore the disappointment filling her. She'd hoped his answer would be slightly different. Their kisses had been spectacular, but maybe that had just been for her. Maybe he hadn't felt the same way. Maybe—

"Wherever you're going, get off the train right now," Tanner said, taking her face in his hands and staring into her eyes. Passion flared in his eyes. "Ninety-ten, Kelly. Ninety percent you. Ninety percent me spending many sleepless nights thinking about how much I like you, how lovely you are. Nights I've dreamed about kissing you and touching you, seeing you naked and hearing you cry out my name as I enter you. You've done more to me with just a couple of kisses than other women have done with a three month affair. I don't know what it is between us, but I do know that it's very special. I want you." He pressed his mouth to hers.

Kelly didn't know what to think. If it was a line, it was a darn good one, and frankly she didn't care.

"I want you, too."

"Good. Now follow me."

He led her over to the blanket. Once there he urged her to sit on the soft fabric. He squatted next to her and opened the bottle of what turned out to be champagne, then poured it into two glasses.

"To us," he said, handing her one.

"To us."

She took a sip. The cool, bubbling liquid teased

her tongue and her throat. She took another sip, then noticed that Tanner hadn't touched his.

"What's wrong?" she asked.

"Nothing. Take another drink."

She did as he asked, but before she could swallow, he kissed her.

She didn't remember setting her glass down but suddenly her arms were around him and his tongue was in her mouth. The tingling bubbles tickled her mouth, while his smooth warmth provided a counterpoint. The combination of champagne and Tanner was the most erotic mixture she'd ever experienced.

He urged her onto her back. She went without protest, wanting him to be close, to touch her everywhere. One hand slipped behind her to unfasten her bra, then the scraps of silk and lace were tossed aside.

"So beautiful," he breathed as he stared at her breasts. He cupped them gently in his hands.

His touch was as wonderful as it had been the previous night, only this time they didn't have to worry about being in a strange house or interrupted by Ryan's children. She let herself relax and savor the sweetness of his gentle caresses as he explored her curves.

He cupped her fullness, then ran his fingers along the underside. He explored the valley between her breasts, all the while kissing her deeply. Her mind split, not sure what to concentrate on more. The sweetness of his mouth on hers, or the magic of his fingers on her breasts? Then there was the whole issue of her hard, aching nipples. Why wouldn't he touch them? The need increased until it was almost pain. Heat, moisture and desire flooded her feminine place making her writhe with longing.

"Tanner," she breathed against his mouth.

"What?"

She opened her eyes and stared at him. Beneath the fire, she saw gentle teasing. "You're tormenting me on purpose."

"Maybe. Do you like it?"

"More than I thought possible."

"But you want me to touch you somewhere else, perhaps?"

"Perhaps."

"What will happen if I do?"

She couldn't help smiling. "It will be very nice."

His face was close to hers. He smiled. "Just nice? I was hoping for more."

"It will be very, very nice."

"Not exactly what I had in mind." He moved his fingers closer, but still didn't touch her nipples.

"Have you thought about what it's going to be like when we're together?" he asked.

She was so lost in the sensations he created that it was difficult to concentrate on his question. "What? You mean while we're making love?"

"Yes." He licked her lower lip. "I have. I've thought about what it's going to be like to be inside of you. I want you. All of you. I want you ready and gasping for me. I want you to welcome me inside of you, then convulse around me. I want you begging and demanding and I want it to be better than anything you've ever experienced before."

He kissed her then, a long, deep, passionate kiss that fuddled her already whirling brain. The images he'd created filled her mind until she felt herself living through the experiences as he'd described them. Combined with the wonder of his kiss and the way his hands felt on her breasts, she found her arousal growing to the point of pain. She needed him desperately. More than she'd needed anyone ever. She'd never been this ready before. Every part of her trembled.

Then his finger moved slightly. She felt the first touch on her tight, aching nipples. He brushed lightly, circled, then squeezed ever so gently. At the same time he slipped between her legs, shifting so he pressed against her. Electricity rocketed through her. Her hips thrust forward, pulsing, pushing her center against his arousal. It didn't matter that they were both wearing jeans. She needed pressure there. Something, anything.

His kiss deepened. She clutched at him, panting, needing. It was too much. It was never going to be enough. She sucked his tongue, held his head in place, then moved one hand lower to his rear and urged him to move faster.

Pressure built between her legs. Pressure and something else. Something almost unfamiliar. Then, before she knew what was happening, before she could do more than catch her breath, she felt a hot jolt of pleasure against that tiny spot of sensitivity. She rubbed against him harder and faster, wanting to feel him. It happened again. His fingers continued to dance on her nipples and the jolt grew and lengthened until it collected itself into an intense release. She shuddered against him. She gasped his name and lost herself in the wonder of the moment.

Tanner continued to kiss her and touch her and with each continued caress, she found her level of need growing instead of easing. The release had only made her want more. She opened her eyes and stared at him.

"I don't understand," she whispered. "What's happening to me?"

"You're very responsive. I can't believe I can make you do that, just by touching your breasts and rubbing against you." He looked two parts proud and one part stunned.

She couldn't believe it, either. Nothing like this had ever happened to her. But she wasn't about to complain. Not when she was still aching to feel him inside of her.

"Tanner, please. I want you."

His eyes darkened to the color of midnight. Without saying a word, he sat up and reached for the snap of her jeans. In less than a minute, he'd pulled off the rest of her clothes and she was lying naked beneath him. Then he tugged off his own sweatshirt.

She stared at his bare, broad chest. In the dim light of the fire, smooth skin glowed. Each muscle defined itself, flexing and relaxing with his movements. When he stood up to pull off his jeans, she found herself trembling in anticipation. She could see the outline of him flexing against the zipper. Then he pushed down his clothes and he sprang free.

He was hard and male and very ready. As he knelt beside her and pulled a condom out of his pocket, she reached over and stroked him. He caught his breath with an audible gasp. His fingers closed on top of her.

"You can't," he told her. "*I* can't. You're too much what I want and I've been thinking about this too long." He drew her hand away.

"Later?"

He flashed her a grin. "Absolutely. I'll even beg you to touch me if you'd like."

She stretched out on her back. "I think I would like that."

He put on a condom, but instead of moving over her, he bent low to kiss her. As his tongue teased her mouth, his hand moved between her legs. She parted for him, welcoming his touch. He explored her slowly, gently, thoroughly, learning the secrets of her body. He slipped through the curls. He searched out that one tiny spot and circled it until her hips pulsed and she gasped and the moment of release was within reach. Then he drew back and moved achingly slowly, around and around, not touching that one spot, but agonizingly close. Circling, teasing, making her plead, finally rubbing it so lightly, so perfectly, she thought she would weep.

The peak crept up on her. It began so slowly, she barely noticed. Then it grew and became so inevitable, the world could have ended and still she would have reached her place of perfection. Then it filled her, reaching deep into every cell, lifting her to another time and place, making her scream, the sound swallowed by his kiss.

While she was still shaking and experiencing absolute wonder, he knelt between her legs and began to fill her.

Kelly felt tears in her eyes. Tears she couldn't explain except to think that they were part of the release. He moved slowly, stretching her, making her cling to him, all the while kissing her.

His weight settled on her, surrounding her, making her feel safe and truly a part of him. He clutched her close, as if he couldn't get enough of her. Fortunately, she could relate to the feeling because despite all he'd done to her already, when he began to move inside of her, it all started again.

With each thrust he carried her higher. She hadn't thought she could experience this and survive, yet she did. Again and again, going deeper and deeper. Her body tensed tighter and tighter until she knew she was going to snap. He moved faster. The world blurred, then disappeared. There was only this man and what he did to her.

She felt him collect himself. Beneath her hands, his body tensed, his hips rocked. They were both going to explode. She could feel it.

He broke the kiss and stared down at her. She looked up at his face, at his eyes, at the uncontrolled passion she saw there.

Later she could not be sure who surrendered first. One minute they were hanging on the edge of eternity and the next they were falling together. She watched exquisite release tighten his features into a mask of passion. She felt her body being torn into millions of points of energy before being reassembled in the most perfect way possible. She heard herself calling out his name, even as he spoke hers.

In the aftermath, when their breathing returned to normal and they were once again able to talk, Tanner cupped her face in his hands. He smiled at her and spoke one word.

"Stay."

She nodded. Tonight there was nowhere else she belonged.

Chapter Thirteen

Kelly leaned her head against Tanner's shoulder. "She's not going to be waking up at night more than another month or so," she said, nodding at the baby in Tanner's arms.

He smiled down at his already dozing child. "I think you're right. She's still eating enough at this feeding that I'm guessing she's waking up because she's hungry and not because of habit, but it won't be all that much longer. We're already down to just one feeding a night."

They were both in Tanner's big bed, up against the pillows. Kelly had to fight against the urge to close her eyes and let herself believe that this was for keeps. Instead she reached out and touched one of Lia's hands.

The little baby closed her fist around Kelly's finger and held on tight. She could smell the fresh scent of baby powder and the male fragrance of Tanner's body. The combination went to her head.

Despite her best intentions, she felt her heart opening to both this man and his child. She wanted to think it was just a reaction to sinus-clearing sex. Anyone would have been shaken by what she and Tanner had just experienced. Except she knew it was more than that.

He was the kind of man women dreamed about. Not just because he was handsome, but because he was strong and kind and caring. How was she supposed to resist a big, tough guy who was willing to change his life to accommodate a new baby? He'd taken Lia even knowing he was going to be a single father. He'd lacked both skills and practical knowledge. He'd been terrified, but he'd done it anyway.

He made Kelly want to lean on him, to borrow some of his amazing strength for her own. She wondered if he would mind, if it was just for a little while. Until she would figure things out for herself.

Lia finished her bottle. Tanner expertly rested the baby on his shoulder and patted her back until she burped twice, then he excused himself to put her back in bed. His quiet confidence was so different from those first few nights when he'd been afraid to do anything. He and his daughter had learned and grown together. They'd bonded. Kelly had known that would happen. But what she hadn't thought was that she might do a little bonding of her own. Somehow, when she wasn't paying attention, she had connected with both Lia and Tanner. She intertwined both her life and her heart with the pair and she didn't know how to separate from them.

The timing was awful, she thought as she slid

down into the bed and pulled the covers up to her chin. She was in no position to get involved with anyone right now. Her life was a mess and she'd just started to notice. There were important issues from her past that she'd ignored. Well, it was time to stop pushing them into the closet. Instead she had to drag them out and stare them in the face.

In the meantime, what was she supposed to do about Tanner?

"She's already asleep," he said as he walked back in the room. He hadn't bothered to pull on clothes and she couldn't help staring at his amazing body. Even as she watched, that most male part of him began to stretch and grow. Her reaction was instinctual and immediate.

She told herself they had things to talk about. There was much she had to explain to him. Tanner slid into bed next to her and gathered her close.

"I know what you're thinking," he said as he pressed his body to hers. "You're thinking that we have to talk about how mature we're both going to be about this change in our relationship. You're thinking that it's going to take time to figure out how to balance this new intimacy with our existing friendship."

His earnest expression made her smile...almost as much as the busy hands caressing her breasts. "Actually, I wasn't thinking that at all, but you're right. We do have to discuss those things."

"I plan to be mature," he told her, reaching for a condom on the nightstand. "I plan to talk about all those things, but first I want to make love again."

As he sank into her, she knew that she'd found an incredibly special man. But she wasn't ready. If she wanted to keep him in her life, she was going to have to do something about getting ready.

His mouth claimed hers. She sighed and welcomed him. Later, she thought hazily as passion overwhelmed. Like Tanner, she would wrestle with this particular demon later.

"Malone," Tanner grunted into the phone. His gaze and his attention stayed focused on the schedule in front of him. They were catching up, but it was a slow process.

"Hi, it's Kelly. How are you?"

Kelly? The familiar voice took about two seconds to settle into his brain, then he was instantly back in his bed, making love with her the way they had at five that morning. The memory made him smile...and get hard.

"Well, hello yourself. This is a surprise." He glanced at his watch. It was a little after three in the afternoon. "Everything all right?"

"I'm fine. I'm here in the hospital with one of my patients."

"You could come and see me in person."

"I wish I could, but she's having twins and they can get complicated. I want to stay close."

"Twins." The thought made him shudder. Lia had been enough of a shock without him having to worry about dealing with two of them. "Good luck."

"Thanks. I'm not expecting any problems, but I want to make sure."

"You're a good doctor."

"Thank you. I appreciate the compliment."

Her voice was soft and appealing, just like her.

He could listen to her for hours. He could do a lot of things with her for hours.

"About last night," he murmured. "Did I tell you how much I enjoyed being with you?"

She laughed. "You might have mentioned it a dozen or so times."

"Good. I want you to know how special our time together was. And incredible."

"I'll say. I didn't even know that my body was capable of responding that way."

She had been remarkably comfortable with him. Tanner wanted to take the credit, telling himself it was his incredible technique or skill, but the reality was he and Kelly simply clicked in bed. He never knew what made that happen. It was some kind of chemistry or emotional connection or a combination of those and other elements. Regardless, he knew that their lovemaking had been extraordinary.

"Do you want to come by after you're done birthing your babies?"

"I'd like to, but I can't."

There was an odd note in her voice. He sat straighter in his chair. "What's wrong?"

"Nothing. I just..." She drew in a breath. "I have to go out of town tomorrow. That's really why I'm calling. I wanted to let you know that I'd be gone."

Something was happening. Tanner could feel it and he didn't like it one bit. "Usually when I don't satisfy a woman in bed she just refuses to see me again. She rarely feels the need to head out of town."

Kelly chuckled. The soft sound relieved him.

"It's not that, and you know it. This isn't even about you."

"Then what's it about?"

"I have a couple of things I have to take care of."

"Business?"

She hesitated. "More like my past. It's just the one day. I'll be back tomorrow night."

"Will you call me when you get back?"

"Would you like me to?" she asked.

"Always."

"Then I will."

He heard a voice in the background.

"I have to go, Tanner."

"All right. You take care of yourself. Have a safe trip."

"I will. Bye."

She hung up the phone.

Tanner slowly lowered the receiver to the cradle, then glanced back at his papers. But instead of seeing the work schedule, he saw Kelly's face, her smile, imagined the way she'd looked that morning when he'd entered her.

She was an amazing woman and he was lucky to have her in his life. Even though he wondered where she was going and what she had to do there, he didn't worry that it had anything to do with another man. He wasn't jealous…yet.

However, it was just a matter of time until Kelly started wondering what she was doing, wasting her time on a guy like him. They were good friends, they were good in bed, but it would never be anything more. Even if he was the type, she wasn't for him. Eventually she would realize that she could do a whole lot better and when that time came, she would leave. Oh, she would want to stay friends for a while, but everything between them would change.

He told himself it didn't matter—that he'd survived without her before and that he could do it again. But the words were empty…as empty as his life had been before she'd entered it and showed him what he was missing.

The cab stopped in front of a pale-white house. As with most residential buildings in San Francisco, this was taller and longer than it was wide. She'd barely had time to step out onto the sidewalk before the front door opened and an older couple came out to greet her.

"Kelly," the silver-haired slender woman said, running lightly down the walkway, her arms open. "It's so good to see you." She enfolded Kelly with a warm hug. "You promised to come visit again, but I didn't think it would take this long to get you back."

"I've been busy," Kelly said.

"We're all busy," Mary Englun told her with a smile. "Life has a way of moving too fast. But you're here now and that's all that matters."

She urged Kelly up the stairs, at the top of which Kelly received an even bigger hug from Mary's husband, Jim. He was a portly man with thinning hair and a smile that brightened a room.

"You're still beautiful as ever," he told her, ushering her inside the lovely home. "Those big eyes are just like Annie Jane's. She's a lucky girl to take after her mother."

"Thank you," Kelly said, feeling both welcomed and awkward.

Mary read her thoughts in an instant. "None of that," she said, patting Kelly's hand. "We're all family. I'll admit it's a little complicated, but that doesn't change the connection." Mary smiled at her. "And it's so good to see you again."

They took Kelly into their living room, a spacious area decorated in green and burgundy. Lush plants grew from pots and hanging baskets. The sofa was large and comfortable. As Kelly took a seat, she saw that Mary had already prepared a pot of tea and several plates of sandwiches and cookies. Mary firmly believed in feeding one's troubles, a philosophy that didn't match her girlish figure.

Mary settled next to her while Jim took a wing chair to her right. "How are things with your practice?" Mary asked as she poured three cups of tea.

"I'm very busy right now. I feel like every woman I see is pregnant. I delivered twins yesterday. A boy and a girl. The babies are healthy and the parents are thrilled, if a little overwhelmed."

"Twins." Jim shook his head. "I'm grateful we had our three one by one."

"Me, too." Mary laughed. "It was hard enough to have all of them in diapers at the same time." She handed Kelly her tea, then passed a cup to Jim.

They chatted a little more about Kelly's practice, then Mary changed the subject. "We told Sara you'd called. She thought about meeting you this time, but the idea still makes her nervous."

"I understand." Kelly didn't tell either of them but she was secretly grateful that her daughter's adoptive mother had stayed away. She wasn't sure she could have handled that meeting right now.

Mary placed her hand on Kelly's forearm. "Annie

Jane is a wonderful child. Most of the time she's thirteen going on twenty-five, but she's still a little girl about some things.''

There was a folder next to the tea tray. Mary opened it and handed Kelly a school photo. A blond, blue-eyed teenager stared back at her. As Jim had mentioned, Annie Jane's eyes were shaped like Kelly's although she got the color from her father. Kelly recognized her smile on the girl, and her hair. She, too, had been blonder when she'd been younger.

So many things were familiar and an equal number strange. Kelly traced the photo and knew that if she and Annie Jane walked down a street together, no one would have trouble placing them as mother and daughter.

"She's doing well in school," Mary said. "Good grades and she's popular. She's not dating yet, but that day is coming. We're all terrified," she added with a laugh. "Boys and hormones. I remember what it was like when Jim and I went through that with our brood.''

Kelly couldn't relate to that, but she knew what she'd been like as a teenager.

"She likes science," Jim put in. He smiled at Kelly. "She wants to be a vet. That commitment to medicine must run in the family.''

"Does she know I'm a doctor?" Kelly asked.

Mary nodded. "Jim and I have told her. Sara doesn't like to talk about you very much, but we've always been available to answer Annie Jane's questions." Mary glanced at her husband. They exchanged an unspoken message.

"I think Annie Jane will want to meet you in a

few years,'' Jim said. "Sara's not going to take it well, so that might delay things, but your daughter is open to the idea.''

Kelly didn't know whether to cry or hug these two very special people. From the very beginning, Jim and Mary had included her as part of Annie Jane's family. They sent regular updates on her progress and even included pictures. Their daughter, Sara, had been unable to conceive, so she and her husband had decided to adopt. But Sara had never been able to face the birth mother of her adored only child. Instead, Jim and Mary were Kelly's connection. They even referred to Annie Jane as *her* daughter. As if she had the right to lay some claim to the child she'd given up at birth.

Mary sorted through dozens more pictures, showing them all to Kelly, letting her pick a couple to take home. Eventually Jim excused himself and the two women were alone.

"It's always lovely to see you,'' Mary said. "But I'm wondering why you came here today.''

Kelly sighed. "I'm not completely sure I have an answer to that,'' she admitted. She looked around the beautifully furnished room. There were framed pictures crowded together above the fireplace and on small occasional tables. Kelly could see Jim and Mary's three, along with the next generation of children. All the pictures were tangible proof that this family prided itself on loving one another.

"Sometimes I just need to be sure that I did the right thing,'' she said at last. "I've been thinking about the adoption a lot lately and I can't help wondering if I was selfish to give up my daughter.''

She looked at Mary. "Please don't think this is

anything about trying to get her back. I would never do that.''

''I know, my dear.'' Mary patted her arm again. ''I just so hate to see you in pain. Why do you doubt your decision?''

''Because—'' Kelly faltered. ''Because I wonder if I should have tried harder. To keep her, I mean. To make it work.''

Mary gestured to the pictures in the room. ''Annie Jane was the most significant gift anyone has ever given this family. You brought my daughter joy. Until she held your baby in her arms, I'd begun to fear for her life. She'd been depressed for over a year. All she'd ever wanted was to be a mother and that was the one thing her body wouldn't let her be. You and Annie Jane saved her. For that I will always be grateful. You weren't selfish, Kelly. You were wise and brave beyond your years.''

Kelly wanted to believe her. ''I didn't feel very brave. I was afraid.''

''Answer me this. Are you a good doctor?''

Kelly nodded. ''Yes. I work hard for my patients and I care about them.''

''So you gave first with your daughter, and now with your choice of career. You're a good person. We can all understand why you did what you did. I suspect you would understand these circumstances in another young woman's life. You would offer her compassion and support. Perhaps it's time to offer the same to yourself.''

Mary's words hit home, but not in the way the other woman had intended. Kelly remembered her conversation with Corina, and how she'd rushed off before reassuring the young woman. Corina's situation was too much like her own for her to be comfortable. Kelly realized that was one time when she hadn't been a good doctor.

"Let go," Mary told her. "Be happy. Find some young man and fall in love. Have more babies, babies that will grow up to be as wonderful as Annie Jane." Tears filled Mary's eyes. "Every time I hold that beautiful girl I'm thankful to you. And I'm grateful to know my granddaughter has such a warm, caring person for her birth mother."

Kelly leaned into Mary's embrace. She let herself absorb the other woman's comforting words. Maybe Mary was right. Maybe it was time to forgive herself and move on.

Plans spilled over Ryan's desk until there wasn't any room for their sandwiches. Tanner pointed to a computer print-out of a calendar. "Angel's ready to start coordinating with your hospital personnel about installation of equipment," he said. "This is the part of the project that's going to get tricky. Everyone thinks his or her department is the most important."

Ryan nodded thoughtfully. "You're going to have a tough time keeping egos in check."

"Agreed. That's why I want Angel in charge. He's going to trample over everyone, which will at least make it fair." Tanner grinned. "Seriously, he's good at this kind of thing. Plus if I stay out of it, he can use me as a point of arbitration when it gets really ugly."

Ryan looked at the calendar, then at the progress report. "You're only about three days behind where you'd initially projected you'd be. I'm impressed. I mean that as your customer. As your big brother, I'm proud as hell.''

''Thanks,'' Tanner said. He'd worked damn hard on this project and it was gratifying to see it come together. ''So how's life as a married man?''

Ryan grinned. ''Great. Next to my kids, Ronni's the best thing that ever happened to me.'' He moved the plans to the side and pulled out his plate. Tanner did the same. Both men took a seat.

Ryan took a bite of his sandwich and chewed. ''There's going to be an adjustment period for everyone. Ronni adores the kids, but face it, they're not easy. They take a lot of time and attention. We're feeling our way through blending the family into a working unit.''

''She loves them.''

''Yeah, she does.'' Ryan smiled, his love for his new wife obvious. ''She's a great mom. Which is good, what with her being pregnant and all.'' He looked back at Tanner. ''We both really appreciate that you helped Kelly out with the kids.''

''It was fun. We had a great weekend.''

''So I heard. Drew said you two did very well for adults unused to being around children.''

Tanner laughed. ''That sounds just like Drew.''

''He also said that you spent a lot of time making eyes at Kelly.''

Tanner concentrated on eating, hoping to avoid an answer. But when Ryan continued staring at him, he knew he wasn't going to get that lucky.

''We're friends,'' he said at last. ''Good friends. We get along.''

''That's not what I heard,'' Ryan teased. ''Rumor has it you're a little bit more than friends.''

Tanner couldn't believe it. How had his brother… Of course. "Ronni."

"Oh, yeah. They were on the phone nearly an hour. Ronni told me later she was gunning for details but Kelly was fairly close-mouthed about all but the big picture." Ryan raised his eyebrows. "So? Now that you've done the wild thing, when are you going to make an honest woman of her?"

Tanner stared at his brother. He doubted he would have been more shocked if Ryan had decked him. "What?"

"Marriage," Ryan said. "You know, long white dress, diamond ring, happily ever after?"

"No way." Tanner swallowed against the tightness in his chest and his throat. "I don't do commitments, at least not like that. Nothing good lasts forever. I'll admit that Kelly's very special and that I'm lucky to have had her in my life, but it's not a forever kind of thing."

Ryan's mouth tightened. "It's time to let go of the past, Tanner. We didn't get many breaks when we were growing up and I can understand why you worry about things lasting, but you're not that scared kid anymore. You're a man. You can take care of yourself."

"It's not me I'm worried about."

"Then who? Kelly?"

He didn't have an answer, so he shrugged. "I told you I don't do permanent."

"So what about Lia? A kid is a pretty permanent fixture in a parent's life. You planning on dumping her in a couple of years?"

"Of course not." Tanner couldn't believe his

brother would even suggest such a thing. "She's my daughter."

"Explain the difference."

Tanner opened his mouth, then closed it. Obviously there was a difference between a wife and a child, but that's not what Ryan was talking about.

Tanner leaned back in his chair and tried to figure it all out. He'd never really put it together before—the forever part. He'd known that Lia was his child and that he'd made the decision to keep her. He'd known it was going to be for a long time, but until this moment, he hadn't realized that he'd signed on for the rest of his life. That no matter what he would be there for her—because he loved her and he no longer wanted to live in a world where she wasn't a part of his life.

He waited for the terror, for the second thoughts and plans for getting away, but none of them appeared. All he felt was a deep and profound love for his daughter.

"Lia is everything to me," he said at last.

"Exactly," Ryan told him. "Loving a child uses a different part of your heart than loving a woman, but the principles are the same. Commitment, patience, time, respect. So I'm going to ask you again. What about Kelly?"

What about Kelly? Tanner didn't have an answer. Because he'd never allowed himself to think of her that way. Not only because of who he was, but because of who she was.

"She's a doctor," he said.

"I've heard that." Ryan's voice was teasing.

"No, I mean she's a *doctor*. I'm just some contractor."

"So this is about what you do for a living?"

"Yeah."

"What about the fact that you love her? Doesn't that count?"

"I don't love her," Tanner insisted, but the words rang hollow. Love? Him? Did he love Kelly?

"You're a fool if you let her go," Ryan told him. "Women like her don't come along every day."

"You think I don't know that? But say you're right. What am I supposed to offer her?"

"Your heart."

"As simple as that?"

Ryan smiled. "It's only complicated if you make it complicated."

Ryan made it sound so easy, but Tanner knew that his brother was wrong. Even if Kelly was the right woman for him, he sure as hell wasn't the right man for her.

Chapter Fourteen

Tanner hesitated outside his front door. Every instinct screamed at him not to go inside.

"You gotta do it, boss," Angel said. "It's not so bad."

Tanner glared at his foreman. "How do you know? Have you done this before?"

Angel shifted uncomfortably from foot to foot. "No, and if I'd kept my big mouth shut, this wouldn't be happening now. But I had to go and mention it to my wife. Gloria got all excited and said she wanted to come, too." He snorted. "As if I would have done this without her."

Tanner completely understood the other man's reluctance. Sure Angel was with him, and Ryan had promised to drop by. Probably just to laugh, Tanner thought grimly. But Kelly had insisted so there was no point in putting off the inevitable.

Tanner sucked in a deep breath and pushed open his front door. At that moment, a gale of female laughter drifted through the house. He shuddered and stepped inside.

The living room was as he'd left it that morning. Still half finished and empty of furniture. But the family room was a different matter. Chairs from the dining room had been pulled in beside the sofas, forming a rough circle. Pink and white streamers fell from the ceiling, while matching balloons had been gathered in bunches and tied to chairs, window sashes and even the refrigerator handle. A dinner buffet covered the counter closest to the family room and he could see the large cake waiting in the dining room. Piles of presents stood by one of the few empty chairs left. Nearly two dozen laughing, talking women sat in the remaining chairs and on the sofa.

If hell was a baby store then purgatory was a baby shower. Why had he let himself be talked into this?

Tanner swallowed hard and thought about retreating. So far no one had seen him. He could make a clean escape and call from his car, claiming a work crisis kept him from attending. But before he could take even one step back, Kelly glanced up and saw him. Then she smiled.

He hadn't seen her much in the past week. First she'd taken her trip to San Francisco to visit her daughter's adoptive grandparents. Then she'd had a couple of emergencies. He'd had a crisis or two of his own and while they'd spoken on the phone, they hadn't had the chance to spend any time together since Sunday night.

Just seeing her sitting there, her wide eyes bright

with humor, her smooth skin begging to be touched, he wanted her. Not just for sex, but also for conversation and even to hold. He'd missed her.

"Tanner!" she called. "You're finally here. We were beginning to wonder."

All the women turned to look at him. He recognized several of his female employees. There was Kelly, of course, and Ronni and Alex, along with wives of some of his employees. Angel made his way to the side of a petite brunette in a business suit.

Tanner gave a general wave and walked to the waiting chair next to Kelly. He couldn't remember a time when he'd been more uncomfortable.

"Isn't this great?" Kelly asked as he sat down. "Everyone came."

"Great. Where's Lia?"

"Napping. She was up a little bit ago and was a hit with your guests."

He wanted to point out that the guests were hers, along with the idea of a baby shower. Why on earth had he agreed?

"We were about to start the games," Ronni said. "Would you like something to drink first?"

"Games? What kind of games?"

His new sister-in-law grinned. "Nothing all that tough. You'll be fine. Why don't I get you some punch?"

As she stood up and started walking toward the kitchen, Tanner had his first chance to notice what the women were eating and drinking. As he did so, his mouth turned down in an involuntary grimace. Everything was pink. The punch, the salad accompanying the small sandwiches, even the cookies.

Now that he thought about it, the cake had been pink, too. Or the icing had been. He didn't dare think about what it would look like when they cut it open.

He leaned toward Kelly. "If I'd had a son, would everything be blue?"

"Of course." She smiled. "Normally the baby shower occurs before the blessed event, so the sex of the child is unknown. But when the shower comes later, or the parents already know the sex, the shower theme reflects that." She patted his hand. "Don't worry. You're going to have a great time. First we'll play a few games, then you can open presents."

"I can't wait," he muttered. "What about the cake?"

"Oh, we'll do that while you're opening presents."

What he really wanted to know was when everyone would be going home. After all, this thing couldn't go on too late, could it? He wanted to spend some time alone with Kelly. He wanted to sit with her and talk, then he wanted to take her upstairs and make love with her.

The front door opened and Ryan walked in. "Over here," Tanner called, feeling the tiniest bit rescued from the situation. "You're just in time for the games."

Ryan looked as puzzled as he had at the mention of games. Then his older brother glanced around the room and started to laugh.

"Don't get too superior about the whole situation," Ronni told him. "When our baby is due, I plan to have a couples shower. That means women *and* men attend.''

Tanner chuckled. ''I'm glad I won't be the only one going through this,'' he said, then had to fight back a groan when Ronni handed him a plastic cup filled with bright pink, foamy punch.

''It tastes better than it looks,'' Kelly said. She waited until Ronni had settled back on the sofa and everyone had moved over to make room for Ryan. ''Let's get started.'' She stood up and walked into the kitchen.

''There are several pads of paper on the coffee table. Take one and pass the rest along until everyone has one. We're going to play the first game.'' She returned carrying a large tray covered by a dish towel.

Tonight she wore her hair up in a twist of some kind. Her long bangs hung to her eyebrows. She didn't go in for makeup but something shiny stained her lips, making Tanner think about licking them clean, then maybe licking her all over. A navy pantsuit emphasized her long legs and slender waist. She was tall and lovely and so much more than he'd ever known in the past. Was she all he'd ever wanted? Was Ryan right about it being time for him to let go of the past?

''The point of the game is to remember as many objects as possible. I'm going to walk around with the tray. No one can start writing until I say so. Are we ready?''

Tanner glanced at Ryan who shrugged.

Ronni grinned. ''To answer that unasked question, yes, of course you two are going to play. The prize is a facial at a beauty salon near the hospital.

If a man wins the game, which is so incredibly unlikely as to not even be worth mentioning, he will give the prize to his significant other.'' She patted Ryan's cheek. ''In your case, that would be me.''

''Thanks for the reminder,'' Ryan grumbled.

Kelly took off the towel and made a slow circuit of the room. Tanner studied the various items. He recognized most of them. A rattle, baby powder, a pair of earrings that Kelly frequently wore, Lia's baby bracelet from the hospital and a condom. The last made him raise his eyebrows, but he didn't say anything. Finally she returned to the kitchen and told them to begin.

Tanner wrote quickly but steadily. He mentally reviewed the tray, going clockwise, filling in the spaces. Had there been two cotton swabs or just one? He figured it didn't really matter. After a couple of minutes, Kelly called time. She asked everyone to count up how many items they had. The person with the most had to read his or her list aloud to verify accuracy.

''Eleven,'' Ronni called out looking smug.

''Fourteen,'' Gloria, Angel's wife, said.

Tanner counted his list again, but didn't say anything.

''How many, Ryan?'' Kelly asked.

''Nine.''

The women all laughed.

''Hey, I got ten,'' Angel called. ''At least I did better than him.''

''How could you remember all that?'' Ryan asked.

Kelly settled her gaze on Tanner. ''What about the proud father? How many do you have?''

He thought about lying, then figured Kelly would probably be able to tell. "Eighteen," he muttered.

There was a collective murmur of surprise.

"Really?" Kelly said. "Want to read them back to me?"

"Sure." He cleared his throat. "A diaper, cotton swabs, an earring, a condom—" Several women laughed.

"Yeah, well, it didn't keep *me* out of trouble," he said, then continued with his list. "Lia's hospital bracelet, baby powder, a rattle, paperclips, a fork, toothpicks, diaper ointment, a sock, lipstick, a car key, a quarter, two theater tickets, a wedding band— Yours, right?" he asked, shooting his brother a look.

Ryan nodded.

"And a pager."

"Wow." Kelly picked up the tray and carried it back into the living room. "The only two things he missed are the washcloth and the battery. Very impressive, Mr. Malone. Looks like you've got yourself one facial."

Which they both knew he'd give to her. "Gee, thanks."

Somehow their gazes got locked together. Even though he told himself to look away, he couldn't. Kelly seemed to be having the same problem.

"I, um, think it's time to cut the cake," she said. "Want to help?"

"Sure."

He excused himself and followed her into the dining room. He knew that they were the center of attention, but right now he didn't care. Instead he pulled her into a corner, out of sight of the family room, and drew her close.

"I've missed you," he told her just before he kissed her.

"Me, too." Her words were muffled against his mouth.

She felt so right in his arms, he thought, needing her more than he thought possible. She wrapped her arms around him and deepened the kiss. He cupped her face and pulled back enough to talk.

"Stay with me tonight," he said. "After the baby shower. I've missed you."

"I've missed you, too." She smiled. "Actually, you'd have to throw me out. I already have an overnight bag in my car."

"I want to hear about what happened when you went to San Francisco."

"Good, because I want to tell you."

The sound of someone clearing her throat made them step apart. Ronni stood in the doorway of the dining room.

"The crowd is getting restless," she said. "I have an idea. Why don't the two of you go back and start opening presents, while I work on cutting the cake."

"Sounds like a plan," Kelly said and led the way.

Tanner settled down in his chair again, but now he didn't feel so very out of place. As he started to open presents, he found himself thinking about the hours that would follow, about how much he wanted to be with Kelly.

Maybe Ryan was right. Maybe it was time to let go of the past and take a chance on the future. Except he was still just a construction worker and Kelly was still a doctor. Did they have a prayer of making it work? What about his fear of losing everything he cared about? Would he survive losing her?

He opened the first box Kelly handed him. It was flat and light, so he guessed clothes. Inside was a frilly yellow dress.

"It's for summer," Mattie, one of his electricians, told him. "So I got the six-month size."

"Thanks. It's very nice. Lia only has one dress right now."

The next box was large and square. He shook it, then glanced at the tag. He recognized Kelly's scrawl.

"You didn't have to get anything," he told her.

"I wanted to. That's half the fun of a shower…buying a baby present."

"That and the pink punch," he said, motioning to his still untouched cup.

He tore off the white and pink paper. Inside was a box with a picture of a lamp. The base was a ballerina teddy bear with a matching shade. He pointed his finger at her. "You're the reason that woman at the store kept telling me this sucker was backordered."

"Absolutely. Once you got serious enough to put up a border print, I knew that Lia had to have the lamp. I bought it about three weeks ago. The woman at the store knew and had been sworn to secrecy."

Ryan leaned forward and handed Tanner a slim box. Inside was a savings bond in Lia's name. "For her college fund," Ryan explained. "It's going to be that time before you know it."

College? His daughter? Of course he wanted her to go, but it seemed so far away. Ryan's gift made him think that the future would be here quicker than he'd realized.

"Look at all this," Kelly said. "Dresses and lamps and money for college. You're turning into a real dad."

She was right. The baby stuff didn't scare him anymore. Nor did his daughter. No matter what happened, he now knew that he and Lia were going to make it. The question was would they make it alone or would someone else join their little family?

"I can't get enough of you," Tanner whispered, his hands buried deep in Kelly's long hair.

She lay beneath him, her naked body all feminine curves and welcoming heat. He could feel her breasts pressing against his chest, and the pressure of her legs wrapped around him, urging him deeper. He was so damn close, but he didn't want to finish…not yet. He wanted their lovemaking to last longer. As it was, they'd barely made it upstairs after the last guest had left. Their clothes lay scattered on the stairs and it was all he'd been able to do to control himself enough to slip on a condom before plunging inside of her.

"Oh, Tanner." She breathed his name with a passionate gasp. She was as responsive this time as she'd been the last.

He'd brought her to climax just by kissing her breasts. When he'd touched between her legs, she'd been so very ready. Slipping one of his fingers inside of her, he'd felt the deep contractions of her muscles as she convulsed around him. Even now, with each thrust, she climaxed, shuddering and clutching, urging him on, to make her do that again.

The problem was watching her react like that was such a huge turn-on that he couldn't hold back. But he had to try. So he forced himself to think of something else. Work maybe or—

She grabbed his buttocks and pressed down, forcing him deeper. She contracted again, milking him. Pleasure built unbearably. He swore, knowing he'd just crossed the point of no return.

"I want you," he growled, then kissed her. He plunged his tongue into her mouth as he plunged his maleness deep inside her. Her movements were frantic, begging, intoxicating. She whimpered.

He moved faster and faster, lost in the moment, feeling himself collect for the ultimate release. Then it was upon him. All he could do was hang on as his body collected itself, then exploded, sending his release rocketing through him. Even as he absorbed the exquisite pleasure, he felt her tightening and releasing as her own climax rippled through her.

They clung to each other until their heartbeats returned to normal. Then he opened his eyes and gazed at her. "Wow."

"My thoughts exactly," she whispered. "How do you do that to me? How do you make me react that way?"

"Just luck."

"Oh, I think it's more than that. Chemistry, maybe."

Or love. But he didn't say that because he wasn't sure. Did he love Kelly? Could he risk it all with her? He touched her face, then gently kissed her mouth. He couldn't imagine her not being a part of his world. She'd entered his life along with Lia and in some ways the two were irrevocably linked in his mind.

"Thank you," he told her.

"Thank *you,* Tanner. It's wonderful to finally get what all the fuss is about."

He rolled onto his side, drawing her with him. "I've missed you."

"Me, too. It's been a long week." She smiled. "I have a lot to tell you. Many things have happened in the past few days."

"Good things or bad things?"

She paused to consider. "Mostly good. I've learned a lot about myself and my past. I went to see—"

A sharp beeping sound filled the room. Kelly sat up. "That's my pager, but where on earth are my slacks?"

"The stairs," he said.

While she went to check her page, he looked in on his daughter. Fortunately Lia had grown accustomed to the sound of Kelly's pager. The baby barely stirred.

Two minutes later he heard Kelly in the hallway. He went out to join her and found her frantically pulling on clothes. "I have to go," she said.

He frowned. "I thought you weren't on call tonight."

"I'm not. It's someone from the clinic. Corina." She looked at him. Her face had gone pale and her eyes were huge. "It's too early. There's something wrong. Dear God, she's only seventeen. She's had enough trouble in her life already—she doesn't need this." She pulled on her shirt and headed down the stairs. "I'm sorry Tanner. I have to be there. I don't have back-up for my clinic patients."

"It's okay. I understand."

She paused at the bottom of the stairs and looked up at him. "Are you sure? I didn't mean to end our evening this way."

"I know. It's fine. Do you want me to drive you to the hospital?"

"No. I don't know how long I'll be." She paused. "I have to go."

And then she was gone. He listened for the sound of the front door closing. After that, there was only silence. Their parting seemed so unfinished. At first Tanner wondered if he was angry with her and just didn't want to admit it. Then he realized it wasn't that at all. What bothered him was what he'd wanted to say as she'd been leaving.

I love you.

He'd wanted to speak the words to her, calling them out as both a talisman and a prayer—for her knowledge and her safekeeping.

I love you. He'd never said those words to anyone before in his life. Women had said them to him and he'd always assumed they were lying.

He turned on his heel and returned to his daughter's room. Even though she was sleeping, he touched her face, then her tiny hand. "Hey, Lia, it's your dad. I just realized something. I've never told you I love you." His throat tightened. "Well, I do. I love you more than I can tell you. I'm going to tell you every single day for the rest of your life." He smiled. "Or at least while you're living under my roof. It'll be hard to say it every day when you're off at college. I want you to know how important you are to me. I want you to know that I'm always going to be here for you." Then he bent over and kissed her.

Finally he returned to his bedroom. Not to sleep, but to wait for Kelly to return.

"She's bleeding," the nurse told Kelly as she scrubbed at the large sink. "The baby is doing all right for now."

Kelly's mind raced frantically as she considered possibilities. "Is the neonatal unit ready for us?" she asked.

"Yes, Doctor."

Kelly stepped away from the sink and headed for the labor room. She had a bad feeling they were going to have to take the baby. A C-section wasn't the end of the world, but it would probably send Corina into a panic. Still, if she was in trouble, there wasn't another choice. No way was Kelly going to lose either of her patients.

"How's it going?" she asked as she stepped into the room.

Corina looked up and tried to smile, but she was crying too hard. "Not great. Something's wrong, Dr. Kelly. I can feel it."

"Your baby wants to come a little early," Kelly said, her voice reassuring. She was frantic to start examining Corina but experience had taught her that thirty seconds of reassurance at the beginning of a problem could literally be a life saver later. "It happens all the time. Some babies are impatient and there's not much we can do about that. But you're well into your thirty-third week. It's manageable."

What was less manageable was the blood she saw

staining the towels that had been tossed into a bucket below the table. Kelly glanced at the monitors attached to Corina and the baby. They didn't have a whole lot of time.

"It's my fault," Corina cried as tears poured down her cheeks. "I know I did something terrible."

"No, you didn't," Kelly told her. "It's not your fault. It just happened."

Big brown eyes bore into her soul. "My baby knows I don't want it. It's trying to die."

Kelly walked over to Corina and took her hands. "You're not doing anything wrong. You and the baby are going to be fine. Do you trust me?"

Corina stared at her, then nodded slowly.

"Good. Now try to relax. I'm going keep both of you safe."

"Doctor?"

Kelly glanced at the monitor, then at the nurse monitoring the bleeding. "Let's get going," Kelly said.

She started issuing orders even as she bent to examine Corina. The rest of the world seemed to fade around her. Her mind cleared. She didn't even have to think, she just knew the next step. She was going to make sure both mother and child came out of this just fine.

Four hours later Kelly stepped into the hallway. It was well after midnight and all she could think about was crawling into bed. The problem was it was too late to go back to Tanner's so she was going to have to crawl into her own bed and sleep alone. Right now that seemed like an empty proposition.

Despite the late hour, there were still people in the hospital corridor. The medical institution never shut down. Which was good news. She could leave knowing that Corina and her baby would be well cared for throughout the night.

"You look exhausted," a familiar voice said.

Kelly glanced up and saw Tanner leaning against the wall. Despite how tired she felt, her heart fluttered in her chest and she couldn't help smiling.

"What are you doing here?"

He shrugged, then walked toward her. "I missed you. I was also afraid you'd get some fool idea that it was too late to come back to my place, so I wanted to be here to tell you that you were wrong. I want you in my bed. To sleep," he amended as he reached out and squeezed her hand. "As much as I'd like to do other things, we both have to get up early in the morning."

She blinked. This wasn't making sense. "You came down here in the middle of the night to see me? Where's Lia?"

"Charming the nurses," he said, jerking his head back toward the nurse's station. "I sneaked her in. So far no one has threatened to call security."

"How long have you been here?"

"About twenty minutes. I called and kept track of how things were going with your patient so I would know when you would be finished." His expression softened. "They told me it was touch-and-go for a while, that you saved the girl's life and her baby's."

"You're not a family member. They wouldn't have given out that information to just anyone."

"I'm not just anyone."

He wasn't. He was someone very special to her, she thought.

"I know it's not my business, or my place, but I'm proud of you, Dr. Kelly Hall. From what I heard, you pulled off a miracle tonight."

He pulled her close and she went willingly into his arms. It hadn't been a miracle but for a while she'd thought she might actually lose them both. Corina had started bleeding even more and then the baby had become distressed. It could have been a disaster, but everything had turned out in the end.

"I had great training," she said. "I knew what to do to save them."

"It was more than that. I overheard a couple of nurses talking. They said that you're gifted. It's as if you know exactly how much more your patients can stand before their strength gives out."

She started to protest, but then she realized he was right. She'd always had the way of sensing the strength of both her mothers and their infants. She loved her work. Tonight wasn't the first time her skill had saved both mother and child.

Kelly pressed her lips together and tried to grasp the significance of what she'd just figured out. She'd saved lives. She was good at what she did—maybe gifted was too strong a term, but she was highly committed and skilled. That counted for a lot. At one time she'd chosen her specialty as a second best—not what she wanted to do, but close. Yet now, after having been in practice for several years, she suddenly understood that this was where she belonged. She was a terrific gynecologist and obstetrician. She had nothing of which to be ashamed.

She wrapped her arms around Tanner's waist and

hugged him tight. "Thank you for being here tonight."

He smiled at her. "I'm not even going to bother saying 'You're welcome.' Where else would I want to be?"

Chapter Fifteen

Despite the fact that she'd only had about four hours of sleep the night before, Kelly was in her office before seven. She had a couple of things to do there before she made her way to the hospital to check on her patients, especially Corina.

Kelly set her purse on her desk, then settled in her chair. She stared at the phone for a long moment before picking it up and dialing a familiar number. With the two hour time difference between Oregon and Kansas, she should catch her father right as he came to work.

"Pastor Hall's office, this is Betty."

"Hi, Betty, it's Kelly. Is my dad around?"

"Kelly!" The older woman's voice rose with a note of both surprise and pleasure. "How are you? Your father says you work too many hours. Is that true? You have to take care of yourself. You're not a teenager anymore. You need your sleep and lots of fruits and vegetables. Did I send you my lentil vegetable soup recipe? It's wonderful. I served it at the ladies prayer lunch just last month and it was a hit. I'll e-mail it to you. Did you know we have e-mail at the church now? Very modern. Horace and I are thinking of getting a computer of our own. The things people can do on those machines. It's just amazing. So why were you calling, dear?''

Despite her exhaustion, her worries and her questions, Kelly couldn't help smiling. Betty never changed. According to town legend, she'd been born talking.

''I'd like to speak to my father.''

''Of course you would. He's right in his office. Just got here a few minutes ago, but then you'd know that. Pastor Hall is as regular as the church clock. He walks through that door every day at exactly eight fifty-eight. In the past ten years I don't know that he's been late more than once, and that was because he stopped to help old Mrs. Winston with her car. It had a flat tire, or was it out of gas? Anyway, he's quite punctual.'' She paused to draw breath. ''I'll let him know you're on the phone.''

There was a click as she was put on hold. Kelly knew that it would be a couple of minutes until her father could get Betty off the intercom so that he could pick up the phone. The older woman was a trial at times, but she was as much a part of Kelly's world as the town where she'd grown up. Betty and Horace had never had children. Despite that, and their differences—her talking constantly and him as silent as a tree—they rarely went anywhere without each other and when they were together, they always held hands. Once when Kelly had been all of fifteen or sixteen, she'd even come across them kissing in a corner of the choir room. It had been the only time she known Betty to be quiet.

"This is an unexpected pleasure," her father said a few minutes later. "Good morning."

"Hi, Dad. How are you?"

"Fine, and according to Betty, I was here right on time, which is a good thing. Otherwise I would have missed your call." He chuckled. "That woman."

"I know she makes you crazy, but you can't get rid of her. She's the only one who understands the filing system."

"Exactly. So what's going on in your life?"

She appreciated that he asked questions rather than assuming a surprise call meant trouble. Her father had always thought the best of her, she reminded herself. He'd always been there for her. Which made the reason for her phone call more difficult.

"I have to ask you something," she said slowly, holding onto the receiver and closing her eyes. She pictured her father, in his shirtsleeves, sitting behind his large desk. "It's about when I was in high school." She cleared her throat. "More specifically, when I got pregnant."

"All right. What would you like to talk about?"

She drew in a deep breath. Her eyes began to burn, but she refused to cry. "I never wanted to disappoint you," she whispered. "I knew what you expected of me and I wanted to do that, but things got out of hand. It was just the one time."

She heard him sigh. "I can't decide if I should

tease you about it only taking one time, or if I should remind you that I love you. I always loved you. And I don't mean that with a silent 'even while you were pregnant' at the end of that sentence. I think I loved you most then because you're my daughter and you were in pain. I suffered with you. In a different way, perhaps, but no less profoundly.''

"Then why did the light go out of your eyes?'' she asked. "Until then, whenever you looked at me, I could see this wonderful light shining from your eyes. I knew that I was the center of your world. But when I told you, the light died. It's never come back.''

"Oh, Kelly, I wish you were here instead of several thousand miles away.''

She gave a soft laugh that was half a sob as well. "So you could beat me?''

He chuckled. Daniel Hall had never once spanked her. The threat of a beating was a private joke between them. "Maybe,'' he teased, then grew serious. "I'll admit that I was shocked to find out about your pregnancy and a little chagrined. After all, you were the pastor's daughter. But that was more about me than you. I thought I knew where you were all the time and what you were doing. It was startling to realize you'd grown up so much. Somewhere along the way my little girl had turned into a beautiful woman and I hadn't noticed. Probably because I didn't want to see. Once you grew up, you would go away and I didn't think I could bear that.''

Two tears escaped her tightly closed eyelids. Kelly groped for the box of tissue on her desk. She wiped her face and sniffed. "I'm sorry, Daddy.''

"No. Don't you dare be sorry. I'm proud of you,

Kelly. Not because you're a doctor, but because of who you are. You're the best daughter ever. Nothing changed for me. The light didn't go out of my eyes, it went out of you. And when it died inside, you couldn't see it in me anymore.''

Her eyes popped open. Kelly stared unseeingly at the wall across the room. ''What?''

''It's true. I've wanted to say something for years now, but it never seemed like the right time. I've watched you punish yourself over and over for something that was never your fault. You were seventeen when you got pregnant and barely eighteen when the baby was born. You had a wonderful dream of being a doctor, and the brains and opportunity to make that happen. Yes, you gave your child up for adoption. Is that so horrible?''

''I don't know.''

''I've spoken with Annie Jane's grandparents just as you have, Kelly. Their daughter was desperate to have a baby. In many ways, you saved Sara. Did it ever occur to you that was the reason you got pregnant? Did you ever stop to think about the gift you gave that family? You can have more children if you choose, but Sara couldn't have any. Every life touched by that child has been blessed. Even yours.''

His words swirled around in her head. She'd never thought of her circumstances this way before.

''You are a gifted healer,'' he continued. ''You've always said that you could have made it if you'd kept the baby. And I'm sure you would have. You're smart and determined. But what would you have done with your life? Would you have gone to medical school?''

"I don't know," Kelly admitted. "It would have taken so long just to get through college, what with working full-time, taking care of a child and taking classes."

"You made a choice. You weren't selfish, you weren't bad, you just made a choice. You gave your daughter to a warm, loving family. There is no evil in that decision. Let it go, Kelly. Forgive yourself. You have been blessed. Stop turning your back on those blessings. Instead, be grateful and move on."

Tears flowed down her cheeks, but they weren't painful or sorrowful, instead they healed her. She felt the empty spots in her heart filling with love and compassion. She felt her spirit lighten, perhaps for the first time in fourteen years.

"You're right," she said simply. "Why didn't I see it before?"

"Because you weren't ready. You had to take the journey to get to your current destination. I love you and I'm proud of you."

Even across half a continent, she felt the warmth of her father's love. It was as if he was with her, holding her close, just as he had when she'd been young. "I love you, too, Daddy."

He was right. The light had always been in his eyes. But she'd been too ashamed to see it shining there. She'd spent years beating herself up for something that deserved to be forgiven a long time ago. If she'd been blind to her father's love for all this time, what else was she having trouble seeing?

"Good morning," Kelly said as she walked into Corina's room. "How are you feeling?"

The teenager smiled wanly. "Better. I slept most of the night."

"The nurses gave you high marks for cooperating," Kelly told her, then pulled up a chair. She would check vital signs in a minute, first she owed her patient an apology.

"Thank you for saving my life," Corina said before Kelly could start talking. "I know it got bad."

Kelly touched the teenager's hand. "I'm glad I was here for you this time, Corina. Because I know I wasn't the last time I saw you, and I'm sorry about that."

Corina raised her bed a few inches. Her braided dark hair spread out on her pillow. Her big eyes widened slightly. "You got paged to the hospital. It was an emergency."

Kelly shook her head. "You're letting me off the hook, and it's not necessary. Yes, I was paged and I had to go then, but you needed to talk. I should have made time later." She squeezed the girl's fingers, then released her hand.

"The reasons are complicated," Kelly said slowly, meeting her gaze. "Your situation reminded me too much of something that had happened in my life. Something that I was afraid to face. I got uncomfortable and it seemed so much easier to hide. So that's what I did."

"I don't understand."

"I know. So I'm going to explain." Kelly quickly recounted the events of her own senior year in high school.

Corina stared in shock. "You gave up a baby for adoption when you were my age?"

"Yes. A little girl. Her name is Annie Jane and

she'll be fourteen this summer. I've kept in touch with her family through her grandparents. For a long time I thought I'd been selfish in giving up my daughter. I thought if I just tried hard enough it wouldn't have been difficult for me to make it work. But I was wrong. I had an opportunity to do something with my life. Something that would make a difference. Something that I desperately wanted. I'm not saying that giving up Annie Jane was easy. I will have to live with the consequences of that decision for the rest of my life. But I don't regret the decision. Knowing what I know now, I would do it all again.''

Corina's eyes widened. ''You wouldn't change anything?''

''Well, I'd forgive myself a little sooner. But aside from that, I wouldn't change a thing.''

Kelly drew in a deep breath and probed her heart. The sense of peace filling her told her that she spoke the absolute truth. She *wouldn't* change a thing about her life. Knowing what she knew now, she would even still have become an OB-GYN, because that was where her talent lay. Her need to be around children would be filled by having a half-dozen kids of her own.

''You have to do what's right for you,'' Kelly told the teenager. ''The other girls in the neighborhood aren't going to live your life. They don't have your scholarship or your drive. Think long and hard before you turn your back on that opportunity. What do you really want for yourself and your child?''

Corina began to cry. Kelly rose and hugged the girl. ''It's okay. You don't have to decide now.''

''I feel so guilty,'' Corina said. ''But I want to

go to college. I spoke to the adoption lady a couple of days ago. She says that there are lots of really great families who want my baby. She'll help me pick the best one." Corina raised her head. Tears spilled out of her eyes. "Am I doing the right thing? Am I being selfish?"

"Not for one second. You are making a tough choice, but it's the right choice for you. I believe in you. If you want, I'll be with you when you choose the family. And I want to stay in touch while you're in college."

She brushed away the teenager's tears. "I even want to help financially. I'll cover whatever expenses the scholarship doesn't. In return, you're going to have to bust your butt to maintain your grades. The only thing I want from you is two promises. The first is that you'll always do your best, and the second is that you'll forgive yourself and instead of feeling guilty, that you'll spend your time counting your blessings."

Corina hugged her hard. "I promise," she whispered. "Thank you, Dr. Kelly. Thank you for everything."

"No problem."

Forty minutes later Kelly left a much relieved Corina watching a morning talk show. The teenager would have to stay in the hospital for another night, then she would be moving into Kelly's tiny apartment. The teenager never wanted to go back to her tenement neighborhood again. Life would be complicated until August, when Corina left for college, but Kelly knew they would figure it out.

She felt as if the weight of the world had been lifted off her shoulders. She was filled with a sense of calm and completeness she'd never experienced before, and her first thought was to share it all with Tanner.

She paused in the hallway. Who would have thought that Tanner could have become a part of her life so very quickly? Two months ago she'd barely known the man existed—and what she did know she didn't like. Now she couldn't imagine her life without him. If she'd ever made a list of what she was looking for, Tanner would be everything she'd ever wanted.

She loved him.

Kelly didn't know when that had first happened, but it was true now. She hadn't just bonded with Lia, she'd also bonded with Tanner. The time they'd spent together, the confessions they'd shared, the lovemaking had bound her to him with a connection that was strong enough to last a lifetime. She wanted to be with him always. She wanted to make a home with him, have children with him, grow old with him.

A quick glance at her watch told her that she would probably catch him in his office right about now. Should she go find him and tell him all that she'd learned, or should she wait? Then she reminded herself that she'd waited long enough already. She'd wasted fourteen years waiting to be good enough, when the answer had been inside of her all along. She was done waiting. It was time to act.

Kelly pulled a hard hat off the table by the entrance to the construction table and followed the large arrows to Tanner's office. He was on the phone when she entered, but he looked up, smiled and motioned for her to take a seat by his desk.

She did as he requested, then removed her hat and smoothed down her hair. Now that she was here, she wasn't so sure what to say.

"Hi," he said when he'd hung up. "I didn't expect to see you this morning. How are you feeling?"

"Tired." She grinned. Despite her physical and emotional exhaustion the night before, when she and Tanner had finally returned to his place and put Lia back to bed, all she'd wanted was to make love. She'd needed to feel him next to her, on top of her, filling her up and making her whole. Now she recognized that she'd needed to express her love, but at the time she'd only known that she needed to fill the yawning emptiness inside.

He stretched. "Me, too. But in a good way. You can keep me awake for that any time you'd like."

She stared at him, at his familiar handsome face, at his blue eyes and his strong body. "I have to tell you something," she said. "I've been doing a lot of thinking. I spoke with my father this morning and with Corina. I finally realized I've been punishing myself for years. I've been living half a life because I didn't feel that I deserved more. I've been so worried about my past that I forgot to think about my future." She sat a little straighter in her chair.

"But all that's behind me now. I've come to understand that if I can forgive other women for the difficult choices they made, I can also forgive myself. I did the best I could at the time. I've gone on to have a successful life doing something that I love. Equally important, my daughter is a happy, healthy, well-adjusted young woman. In time she may want to meet me, or she may decide against that. Either choice is hers. I have promised myself to be as understanding of her as my father was of me.''

Tanner stared at her. "You *have* been working through a lot.''

She nodded. "I'm done punishing myself. I've decided to go after what I want.''

He didn't move, but she sensed his withdrawal from the conversation as surely as if he'd stepped out of the room. "What's wrong?''

"Nothing. I'm happy for you.'' His words sounded sincere, but the bleak expression in his eyes didn't change. "It's just that I'm going to miss you. I've gotten used to having you around. I didn't think we had anything permanent, but I also hadn't figured on you leaving just yet.''

Kelly told herself not to jump to conclusions. Just as she had issues from her past to come to terms with, Tanner had the same. She took a calming breath before speaking.

"I'm not going anywhere, Tanner. I'm willing to give you as much time as you need to learn to trust me.''

"Oh, I do trust you. You've been a great help to Lia and me.'' He leaned forward and placed his hands on the table. "You're an amazing woman. In time you're going to want to find the right kind of man. Maybe another doctor or a lawyer. Someone professional. Someone—''

"I love you,'' she said, interrupting. "I don't want anyone else.''

He stiffened. The bleakness left his eyes, but she couldn't read was he was thinking. "You say that now, but it's because of last night. Eventually—''

She rose to her feet and walked around the table until she stood next to him. "Eventually I'm still going to love you. Not a doctor or a lawyer or anyone else. Just you. I love you, Tanner. And Lia. I love both of you."

He stood up with such force that his chair went skidding back and bumped into the wall. "Dammit, Kelly, I'm trying to be noble here."

"Why?"

"Because you deserve better."

She gathered up all her courage. Here it was—the moment of truth. Was she really going to say what she was thinking? Was she, for once in her life, going to go for it?

"Could anyone love me more or better than you do?" she asked.

She watched him wrestle with his demons. Uncertainty, longing, pain, mistrust, then need, all chased across his face. She knew about his past, about the ways he'd been let down. She knew how difficult it would be for him to let himself believe that someone was always going to be there for him. She knew about his pride, his strength and the small dark place he kept hidden in his soul.

He reached out and stroked her cheek. "No one could love you more than I do," he said hoarsely. "Or better. You are my life, my world. I don't want anyone else in my bed or my arms. You're the one I want. For me, for Lia, for the children I want to have with you."

He motioned to the unfinished room. "This is what I am. This is what I do. Is it enough?"

He was fiercely intense, his passion and love

burning hot inside of him. She loved everything about him. She took his hands in hers.

"You are more than enough—just as you are. You are the light shining in the darkness of my soul, and I am the same for you. I've waited all my life to find you, Tanner Malone. Don't for a moment think I'm going to let you go."

He pulled her close and kissed her. The familiar feel of his body was enough to make her melt against him. Nothing had ever been as right as being with him.

"So when do you want to get married?" he asked.

She laughed. "Not if, but when?"

He stared at her. "When," he repeated firmly. "I'm not letting you get away, Kelly. I love you too much as it is."

"I'm guilty of that, too," she said. "Yes, I'll marry you. Whenever you'd like."

"How about after the hospital dedication? Then we can take time off and have a real honeymoon."

He kissed her again. She was having trouble thinking as he worked his magic on her. She pulled back enough to ask, "What about the wedding. Isn't that important as well?"

"Very important. Just don't make me eat a pink cake."

"I promise."

He stared at her. "I'll love you forever."

"I know." That was the best part, she thought as she hugged him close. She did know.

Epilogue

The crowd was definitely louder. Tanner and Kelly moved in time with the music, but it was impossible to talk over the noise.

"This is getting out of hand," she said into his ear. He barely heard her.

"Tell me about it. But they're having a great time."

He glanced around his brother's living room. The large area was crammed with well-wishers. Despite the fact that they'd pulled together an engagement party less than two weeks after they'd decided to get married, the turn-out had been huge. It seemed as if everyone in their lives wanted to wish them well.

Tanner had already met Corina, the pretty young teenager Kelly was going to mentor, and Daniel, Kelly's father. The minister had been warm, welcoming Tanner to the family. Tanner had sensed immediately that they were going to be good friends as well as in-laws.

He felt a tap on his shoulder. "Don't even think about it," he said, turning to glance at his brother. "No one dances with my fiancée except me."

But Ryan wasn't smiling. "I need to speak to you for a second," he said.

"Go ahead," Kelly told him, already stepping back. "I want to get something to drink. I'll catch up with you in a couple of minutes."

Tanner nodded, then followed Ryan into the study. His brother shut the door. Instantly the noise level dropped considerably.

"What is it?" Tanner asked. When Ryan didn't answer, Tanner got a bad feeling in the pit of his stomach. "Don't tell me there's another problem with the funding."

"Nothing like that," Ryan assured him.

"Then what?"

Ryan pointed to the phone receiver resting on the desk blotter. "We have a call," he said. "It's from a man claiming to be our long lost brother."

* * * * *

To find out more about Ryan and Tanner's long lost brother, be sure to look for Christine Flynn's
DR. MOM AND THE MILLIONAIRE
the wonderful conclusion to
PRESCRIPTION: MARRIAGE
available from Silhouette Special Edition on sale in February

A Note From the Author

I was thrilled and excited when I learned our wonderful editors at Silhouette Special Edition were interested in Christine Flynn, Christine Rimmer and myself writing more Prescription: Marriage books. My first one, PRINCE CHARMING, M.D., had been so much fun to write and the "two Chris's" and I worked very well together.

Creating characters for a series is always a challenge. While each hero and heroine needs to be unique for each story, there also have to be elements which link everyone together. The first Prescription: Marriage novels had three friends who were nurses as well as heroines. This time we decided to go a little deeper. Not only are our heroines good friends and doctors, but two of our heroes are brothers while the third is...well, that's a surprise to be revealed in the third book—DR. MOM AND THE MILLION-AIRE, out next month!

We added children to the mix in this new series. In the first book, A DOCTOR'S VOW, Ryan Malone had three children of his own. Kids are fun to write about because they always get the best lines. In THEIR LITTLE PRINCESS, Tanner finds himself the father of a newborn…with about twenty-four hours notice. The third book of the series, DR. MOM AND THE MILLIONAIRE, has a four-year-old Tyler charming the socks off everyone.

Children add a special dimension to any romantic relationship. Children up the stakes, add complications and often give the very best hugs. We all enjoyed our time with our wonderful heroes and heroines, and their extended families.

So, welcome to the continuation of Prescription: Marriage, part two. We promise lots of love, laughs, those steamy bits and plenty of hugs for all.

Back by popular demand!

CHRISTINE RIMMER
SUSAN MALLERY
CHRISTINE FLYNN

prescribe three more exciting doses of heart-stopping romance in their series, **PRESCRIPTION: MARRIAGE.**

Three wedding-shy female physicians discover that marriage may be just what the doctor ordered when they lose their hearts to three irresistible, iron-willed men.

Look for this wonderful series at your favorite retail outlet—

On sale December 1999:
A DOCTOR'S VOW (SE #1293)
by **Christine Rimmer**

On sale January 2000:
THEIR LITTLE PRINCESS (SE #1298)
by **Susan Mallery**

On sale February 2000:
DR. MOM AND THE MILLIONAIRE (SE #1304)
by **Christine Flynn**

Only from
Silhouette Special Edition

Visit us at www.romance.net

SSEPM

If you enjoyed what you just read,
then we've got an offer you can't resist!

Take 2 bestselling
love stories FREE!
Plus get a FREE surprise gift!

Clip this page and mail it to Silhouette Reader Service™

IN U.S.A.	**IN CANADA**
3010 Walden Ave.	P.O. Box 609
P.O. Box 1867	Fort Erie, Ontario
Buffalo, N.Y. 14240-1867	L2A 5X3

YES! Please send me 2 free Silhouette Special Edition® novels and my free surprise gift. Then send me 6 brand-new novels every month, which I will receive months before they're available in stores. In the U.S.A., bill me at the bargain price of $3.57 plus 25¢ delivery per book and applicable sales tax, if any*. In Canada, bill me at the bargain price of $3.96 plus 25¢ delivery per book and applicable taxes**. That's the complete price and a savings of over 10% off the cover prices—what a great deal! I understand that accepting the 2 free books and gift places me under no obligation ever to buy any books. I can always return a shipment and cancel at any time. Even if I never buy another book from Silhouette, the 2 free books and gift are mine to keep forever. So why not take us up on our invitation. You'll be glad you did!

235 SEN CNFD
335 SEN CNFE

Name	(PLEASE PRINT)	
Address	Apt.#	
City	State/Prov.	Zip/Postal Code

* Terms and prices subject to change without notice. Sales tax applicable in N.Y.
** Canadian residents will be charged applicable provincial taxes and GST.
  All orders subject to approval. Offer limited to one per household.
  ® are registered trademarks of Harlequin Enterprises Limited.

MONTANA MAVERICKS
Big Sky Brides

Legendary love comes to Whitehorn, Montana,
once more as beloved authors

Christine Rimmer, Jennifer Greene and Cheryl St.John

present three brand-new stories in this exciting anthology!

Meet the Brennan women:
SUZANNA, DIANA and ISABELLE

Strong-willed beauties who find unexpected
love in these irresistible marriage of
covnenience stories.

Don't miss
MONTANA MAVERICKS: BIG SKY BRIDES
On sale in February 2000,
only from Silhouette Books!

Available at your favorite retail outlet.

PSMMBSB

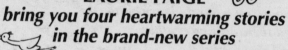

Don't miss Silhouette's newest cross-line promotion,

Four royal sisters find their own Prince Charmings as they embark on separate journeys to find their missing brother, the Crown Prince!

The search begins in October 1999 and continues through February 2000:

On sale October 1999: **A ROYAL BABY ON THE WAY**
by award-winning author **Susan Mallery** (Special Edition)

On sale November 1999: **UNDERCOVER PRINCESS**
by bestselling author **Suzanne Brockmann** (Intimate Moments)

On sale December 1999: **THE PRINCESS'S WHITE KNIGHT**
by popular author **Carla Cassidy** (Romance)

On sale January 2000: **THE PREGNANT PRINCESS**
by rising star **Anne Marie Winston** (Desire)

On sale February 2000: **MAN...MERCENARY...MONARCH**
by top-notch talent **Joan Elliott Pickart** (Special Edition)

ROYALLY WED
Only in—
SILHOUETTE BOOKS

Available at your favorite retail outlet.

Visit us at www.romance.net

SSERW

SILHOUETTE'S 20TH ANNIVERSARY CONTEST
OFFICIAL RULES
NO PURCHASE NECESSARY TO ENTER

1. To enter, follow directions published in the offer to which you are responding. Contest begins 1/1/00 and ends on 8/24/00 (the "Promotion Period"). Method of entry may vary. Mailed entries must be postmarked by 8/24/00, and received by 8/31/00.

2. During the Promotion Period, the Contest may be presented via the Internet. Entry via the Internet may be restricted to residents of certain geographic areas that are disclosed on the Web site. To enter via the Internet, if you are a resident of a geographic area in which Internet entry is permissible, follow the directions displayed on-line, including typing your essay of 100 words or fewer telling us "Where In The World Your Love Will Come Alive." On-line entries must be received by 11:59 p.m. Eastern Standard time on 8/24/00. Limit one e-mail entry per person, household and e-mail address per day, per presentation. If you are a resident of a geographic area in which entry via the Internet is permissible, you may, in lieu of submitting an entry on-line, enter by mail, by hand-printing your name, address, telephone number and contest number/name on an 8"x 11" plain piece of paper and telling us in 100 words or fewer "Where In The World Your Love Will Come Alive," and mailing via first-class mail to: Silhouette 20th Anniversary Contest, (in the U.S.) P.O. Box 9069, Buffalo, NY 14269-9069; (In Canada) P.O. Box 637, Fort Erie, Ontario, Canada L2A 5X3. Limit one 8"x 11" mailed entry per person, household and e-mail address per day. On-line and/or 8"x 11" mailed entries received from persons residing in geographic areas in which Internet entry is not permissible will be disqualified. No liability is assumed for lost, late, incomplete, inaccurate, nondelivered or misdirected mail, or misdirected e-mail, for technical, hardware or software failures of any kind, lost or unavailable network connection, or failed, incomplete, garbled or delayed computer transmission or any human error which may occur in the receipt or processing of the entries in the contest.

3. Essays will be judged by a panel of members of the Silhouette editorial and marketing staff based on the following criteria:

> Sincerity (believability, credibility)—50%
> Originality (freshness, creativity)—30%
> Aptness (appropriateness to contest ideas)—20%

Purchase or acceptance of a product offer does not improve your chances of winning. In the event of a tie, duplicate prizes will be awarded.

4. All entries become the property of Harlequin Enterprises Ltd., and will not be returned. Winner will be determined no later than 10/31/00 and will be notified by mail. Grand Prize winner will be required to sign and return Affidavit of Eligibility within 15 days of receipt of notification. Noncompliance within the time period may result in disqualification and an alternative winner may be selected. All municipal, provincial, federal, state and local laws and regulations apply. Contest open only to residents of the U.S. and Canada who are 18 years of age or older, and is void wherever prohibited by law. Internet entry is restricted solely to residents of those geographical areas in which Internet entry is permissible. Employees of Torstar Corp., their affiliates, agents and members of their immediate families are not eligible. Taxes on the prizes are the sole responsibility of winners. Entry and acceptance of any prize offered constitutes permission to use winner's name, photograph or other likeness for the purposes of advertising, trade and promotion on behalf of Torstar Corp. without further compensation to the winner, unless prohibited by law. Torstar Corp and D.L. Blair, Inc., their parents, affiliates and subsidiaries, are not responsible for errors in printing or electronic presentation of contest or entries. In the event of printing or other errors which may result in unintended prize values or duplication of prizes, all affected contest materials or entries shall be null and void. If for any reason the Internet portion of the contest is not capable of running as planned, including infection by computer virus, bugs, tampering, unauthorized intervention, fraud, technical failures, or any other causes beyond the control of Torstar Corp. which corrupt or affect the administration, secrecy, fairness, integrity or proper conduct of the contest, Torstar Corp. reserves the right, at its sole discretion, to disqualify any individual who tampers with the entry process and to cancel, terminate, modify or suspend the contest or the Internet portion thereof. In the event of a dispute regarding an on-line entry, the entry will be deemed submitted by the authorized holder of the e-mail account submitted at the time of entry. Authorized account holder is defined as the natural person who is assigned to an e-mail address by an Internet access provider, on-line service provider or other organization that is responsible for arranging e-mail address for the domain associated with the submitted e-mail address.

5. Prizes: Grand Prize—a $10,000 vacation to anywhere in the world. Travelers (at least one must be 18 years of age or older) or parent or guardian if one traveler is a minor, must sign and return a Release of Liability prior to departure. Travel must be completed by December 31, 2001, and is subject to space and accommodations availability. Two hundred (200) Second Prizes—a two-book limited edition autographed collector set from one of the Silhouette Anniversary authors: Nora Roberts, Diana Palmer, Linda Howard or Annette Broadrick (value $10.00 each set). All prizes are valued in U.S. dollars.

6. For a list of winners (available after 10/31/00), send a self-addressed, stamped envelope to: Harlequin Silhouette 20th Anniversary Winners, P.O. Box 4200, Blair, NE 68009-4200.

Contest sponsored by Torstar Corp., P.O. Box 9042, Buffalo, NY 14269-9042.

ENTER FOR
A CHANCE TO WIN*

Silhouette's 20th Anniversary Contest

Tell Us Where in the World
You Would Like *Your* Love To Come Alive...
And We'll Send the Lucky Winner There!

Silhouette wants to take you wherever
your happy ending can come true.

Here's how to enter: Tell us, in 100 words or less,
where you want to go to make your love come alive!

In addition to the grand prize, there will be 200
runner-up prizes, collector's-edition book sets
autographed by one of the Silhouette anniversary
authors: **Nora Roberts, Diana Palmer,
Linda Howard** or **Annette Broadrick**.

DON'T MISS YOUR CHANCE TO WIN!
ENTER NOW! No Purchase Necessary

Where love comes alive™

Name:

Address:

City: State/Province:

Zip/Postal Code:

Mail to Harlequin Books: **In the U.S.:** P.O. Box 9069, Buffalo, NY
14269-9069; **In Canada:** P.O. Box 637, Fort Erie, Ontario, L4A 5X3

COMING NEXT MONTH

#1303 MAN...MERCENARY...MONARCH—Joan Elliott Pickart
Royally Wed
In the blink of an eye, John Colton discovered he was a Crown Prince, a
brand-new father...and a man on the verge of falling for a woman in *his*
royal family's employ. Yet trust—and love—didn't come easily to this
one-time mercenary who desperately wanted to be son, brother,
father...*husband?*

#1304 DR. MOM AND THE MILLIONAIRE—Christine Flynn
Prescription: Marriage
No woman had been able to get the powerful Chase Harrington anywhere
near an altar. Then again, this confirmed bachelor had never met someone
like the charmingly fascinating Dr. Alexandra Larson, a woman whose
tender loving care promised to heal him, body, heart...and soul.

#1305 WHO'S THAT BABY?—Diana Whitney
So Many Babies
Johnny Winterhawk did what any red-blooded male would when he found
a baby on his doorstep—he panicked. Pediatrician Claire Davis rescued
him by offering her hand in a marriage of convenience...and then showed
him just how real a family they could be.

#1306 CATTLEMAN'S COURTSHIP—Lois Faye Dyer
Experience made Quinn Bowdrie a tough man of the land who didn't need
anybody. That is, until he met the sweetly tempting Victoria Denning, the
only woman who could teach this stubborn rancher the pleasures of
courtship.

#1307 THE MARRIAGE BASKET—Sharon De Vita
The Blackwell Brothers
Rina Roberts had her heart set on adopting her orphaned nephew. But the
boy's godfather, Hunter Blackwell, stood in her way. Their love for the
child drew them together and Rina knew that not only did the handsome
doctor hold the key to Billy's future—but also to her own heart.

#1308 FALLING FOR AN OLDER MAN—Trisha Alexander
Callahans & Kin
Sheila Callahan dreamed of picket fences and wedding rings, but
Jack Kinsella, the man of her dreams, wasn't the slightest bit interested in
commitment, especially not to his best friend's younger sister. But one
night together created more than just passion....